Flying Goats in Agadir

Kirstin Ruth Bratt

First published 2016 by Dahlia Publishing Ltd
6 Samphire Close Hamilton
Leicester LE5 1RW
ISBN 9780956696779

A CIP catalogue record for this book is
available from The British Library

Acknowledgments

I imagine most books come from a community of support, and this book is certainly one of those. My own children, Sha-Narah and Gabriel, who sacrificed too much for this project, are the two to whom I owe the greatest debt. I love these sweet and wonderful children more than they could ever know.

This book began as two separate projects, neither of which came into being – a travel guide to Morocco and an ethnography of Moroccan festivals. It was Jonas Elbousty who worked with me on the original manuscripts and who interviewed many of the people in the villages who planted the seeds for what became fictionalized here. Much of the information in this book was gathered with him, and certainly this book would not have existed without him. Also, he introduced me to his country from the mountains to the deserts, from every border to every coastline. Without him and his very gracious family, this book would never have come into being.

Thanks very much to the communities of Al Akhawayn and Ibn Zohr universities for their many gestures of kindness.

Also, a number of editors gave me the chance to publish short excerpts of this novel. Thanks to Driss Ouaouicha of Al Akhawayn University; Heather LeFebvre, *Broad! Magazine*; Oksana Tovmachenko, *Kite Journal*; Jo Slade, *Stony Thursday Book*; Tilly Craig, *Tribe*; Robert Kotchen, *Labletter*; Brentley Frazer, *Retort*; Linda Blaskey, *Broadkill Review*; Arup Chatterjee, *Cold Noon*; Pradeep Chaswal, *Muse*; M. F. Macpherson & Tom Holmes, *Redactions*; Christopher Anderson and Jenn Monroe, *Extract(s)*; Tara Masih, *Thumbnail*; Leila Rae, *Riverbabble*; Adnan Mahmutovic, *Two-Thirds North Anthology*; Libby Walkup, *Ginger Piglet Press*; Darin Beasley, *Marco Polo*; M. P. Jones, *Kudzu Review*; and T. S. Tsonchev,

Montreal Review. Thanks to Arteles Creative Center, in Hameenkyro, Finland; Southeastern Wisconsin Festival of Books; Lake Region Writers Network; the American Comparative Literature Association; Zaytoun School of Tamri; the Souss-Massa-Draa Academy, the World Justice Project, and the Association of Writers and Writing Programs.

Thanks to the American Institute for Maghrib Studies, whose original fellowship made our research possible. For awards and recognitions along the way, thanks to the Brainerd Writers Alliance, Northwoods Writers Conference, and the Muslim Writers Awards of the UK. For her keen eye and insights, thanks to Doreen Bultema Wolfgram. Thanks also to Yahya Fredrickson, Victoria Tirrel, and Beth Browne for their comments.

When Farhana Shaikh first contacted me about publishing this book, I was moved by her deep understanding of these characters, who came to life under her guiding hand. Farhana is a gentle and thoughtful mentor who can see into the heart of things. I will be ever grateful.

Prologue

Asalam 'alaykum.

There may be other ways to greet you, but this is my favourite. This hello is filled with love – and not only for you, the person I address directly, but for you in plural – the many others, whether present or absent, who love you – your family, your community, your knowns and unknowns. The last Prophet of Islam, may he rest in peace, is Mohammed, a shy, unassuming, and humble man – one who went without food so that the hungry would eat, who took widows and orphans into his family, who fought and wrestled with an angel, who asked God to find someone else to be his prophet, someone more outspoken and clear, or more studious. But God insisted on Mohammed, they say, not because of a reputation with the scholars but because of his reputation with everyone else – because his well-known honesty and perseverance would be convincing among the sceptical. And finally, Mohammed relented into his role as a prophet, reminding us always to be kind and peaceful with one another, to be devoted to a spiritual journey on earth, and to remind one another frequently how to coexist in peace and equality, to put the needs of one's community above one's selfish concerns. The greeting is a continual reminder:

Asalam 'alaykum – peace to you and all those who are with you.

Moroccan hospitality

I want to dispel a few notions. Foremost is this: there is no magic in Morocco. There may be snake charmers in Marrakesh and monkeys wandering close to you in the forests of Azrou; there may be flying goats in the argan trees by Taroudant. Who knows? There may even be jinns. There are storytellers in the main squares who can captivate the attention of an audience night after night. But in Morocco, there isn't any magic – only things that cannot be explained.

As an anthropologist, my work requires travel, often to places less travelled, and this is the case with my beloved as well. Our travels are not only the basis of our stories but also of our careers. As often happens with people who travel to interesting places, we were drawn to anthropology, and when we met, both engaged in our fieldwork, we came easily to understand one another. At first it was our work that drew us together; soon it was a mutual attraction we felt for one another.

The job of the anthropologist is to stay above the fray, to listen to all and be unduly influenced by none, to witness the drama of daily life without creating any drama in our own. For the most part, at least in the field, we are successful in this.

Department politics, though. That's where we find our drama. The truth is that scholarship in any discipline requires a measure of arrogance and self-importance. Some say it requires a touch of insanity to hold to the idea that we can remain free of bias or that our basic theories are inviolable and imperturbable.

The blind spot of a scholar can be a small fleck or a gaping hole: it is born in youthful ideals, false readings of our predecessors, untested and shaky hypotheses; it is steeped in our most closely held certainties.

Such blind spots can be easily covered or concealed at first, before we are cited or challenged in public venues. Scholarship is like the construction of a building: we select our foundation and begin to build a structure thereupon. It should have a strong and defensive design because a scholar spends a lifetime securing it.

As we reach our middle and advanced years, younger scholars (even — no, especially — our closest advisees) begin to take their shots, dissolving our weakest parts first. They come merciless and crushing because they will make a career of discrediting their elders. The building may be sweet and quaint or a mighty fortress — it hardly matters; any slight failing or hint of disorder will cause it to fall, crashing and tumbling to the ground in a heap.

This construction and destruction — this is what happens to the tenured professor. This is the process we cheer and encourage in university life. My beloved and I find ourselves in the same devastating cycles — between building our own castles and attacking the others. Our drama is out of proportion with the world outside.

In the field of anthropology, there are the gregarious and active, those who easily fit into any environment, and there are the quiet note-takers who sit on the sidelines and gather information. My beloved is of the former type, while I am of the latter. In this way, our joint projects are thorough and complete.

My need for solitude is my greatest liability as an anthropologist, but I can put it aside in the earliest hours of the day. In the mornings, I am an enthusiastic student of human nature, anxious to gather information. In a foreign place, I am learning the language, desperate to soak in all the new words and quickly put them to use, certain that the key to knowledge is just behind that wall of new words before me. By evening, though, my curiosity fades, and the strain of my limited vocabulary is enervating.

In the States, there is nothing wrong with being detached and quiet. I can make brief visits and brief phone calls, and no one takes offence at my brevity. Sometimes I allow years to pass without contacting someone, even a dear friend or cousin I care for deeply and think of often. In Morocco, though, a place of hosting and being hosted, I am expected to adapt to a community. My personality cannot become an obstacle in my work. I cannot say, "This is just my way" or expect anyone to accept me as I am.

As an anthropologist, I have certain responsibilities – to be patient, put my own desires to the side, and adjust to situations. I must remain aware that my nation's image abroad, especially in Muslim nations, is troubled, and I have an opportunity to improve it. As people abroad, we can do a small part to rectify global misunderstandings, and why not? We can do a world of good as people abroad.

I also consider that my responsibility to my host nation is to encourage its best traditions. Morocco is a place of great beauty and kindness, a place of neighbourly traditions and thoughtful gestures, a place where people show faith in God, faith in one another. It is a gift to be in such a place. As a guest, I should participate in the reciprocal agreements of the community, an obligation that is larger than I am, larger than my own small emotional climate.

Yet even knowing all this, I suffer limitations. My beloved and I have misunderstandings when it comes to hosting and being hosted. My lethargy about visiting is a problem for him: not in the States, where he shares my desire to sequester ourselves with our work. In Morocco, though, he is not only an anthropologist but also a family member. When we do field work in Morocco, our family understands our need to work during the day, but they want to see us in the evenings. When we respond to invitations, his manners are always superior to mine, and his patience stretches from one person to another in his effort to accommodate all.

This is how it happens: we receive an invitation towards the end of an exhausting day. I say to him, let's rest here alone, but even I know this is impossible. We agree to go for a short time, but we know this is impossible too. It is only something we say to one another, and not a serious commitment.

In Morocco, hosting is a complex and prolonged process. A host wants to provide a complete experience: a memorable meal, stimulating conversation, and a place of rest and respite. Not only a meal, a feast! Our host wants us to eat until we cannot possibly eat another delicious bite of lamb and chicken and soup and sweets. Not only that: when we think we are finished, our host will offer our satiated bodies another delicious pastry or a pile of fruit – then tea – then more sweets. Our host will go to great expense – we know this – will be warm and loving and kind throughout this meal, will treat us as monarchs, as if our eating is a favour.

You may wonder, when you first sit down to one of these sumptuous feasts, how much to eat at each course. One method is to count the tablecloths and divide your hunger accordingly, but this method is unreliable, as some courses aren't messy enough to warrant a separate cloth. So be aware, as the first course appears before you, there is more to come. Much more. I remember well my first

Moroccan meal, when I ate all I wanted at the first course. It is easy to do, but don't. Imagine a grand banquet still waiting to be served behind the dining room wall, and eat with moderation.

No host will ever warn you to temper your eating; this is why I am warning you here. Your generous host will delight in surprising you with gorgeous platters of food and will encourage you to eat heartily at every serving. By all means, eat! Keep chewing, but slowly: people are watching to ensure your happiness and satisfaction. As a newcomer in Morocco, you may be given your own plate, even if others eat from a common platter. My beloved and I always prefer to eat from the common dish, but this decision is entirely yours. Your host just wants you to be comfortable.

One evening of Ramadan, my beloved and I are invited to break the fast at the home of one marvellous woman, Kawthar, and her lovely family. Kawthar is a sweet, angelic, darling woman. If she had been born in ancient Greece, she would have taken the nectar of the gods and improved upon the recipe. She employs an assistant to help her, but it is Kawthar who reigns in the kitchen. On our way to her house I remind myself to eat slowly, to relish each bite; I know how I exaggerate at Kawthar's table.

The breaking of the fast begins with a brief prayer of thanks for our day of fasting and remembrance – then a date and drink of water. We eat this first morsel slowly, savouring its sweetness. Then it is time for prayers before the meal truly begins. These prayers are the sweetest part of Ramadan, a meditation on all God's gifts and mercies. After prayer come cakes, breads, fruits, juices, and nuts, followed by luxurious pastilla – a flaky crust filled with pigeon, seafood, eggs, and spices – that we carefully pull apart with our hands from the common platter. Then a tagine of chicken, another of beef, then more fruits, tea, coffee, and sweets until we are so full we can hardly rise from our seats, satiated and heavy, but no matter. No one obliges us to move.

From the moment we arrive until the final parting moments, we can't be in need of a thing: just as I think of a napkin, I look up to find one held out for me. Someone places soft and delicious chicken before me, while another is filling my glass. A chunk of bread appears at the moment I wish for it. What is remarkable about Moroccan hosting is how natural it all seems. An incredulous guest will observe spectacular displays of kindness – so much as to make one feel an inconsiderate dolt, except that no Moroccan host would allow such a thought. The host will sense each of your emotions and allow for only the happiest to stay.

I often wonder at this seemingly intuitive ability, especially when I look over to see a young child reaching towards me with a platter of pastries or a toothpick. Is it possible that even a young person can anticipate their guests and provide for the subtlest of whims? Is this a natural ability or is it taught? It can't be natural because it would be universal, but if it is taught, then how? Are Moroccan children given explicit lessons on the essentials of good hosting? At what age does this begin? How can it be possible?

I wonder this time and again, how my host knows exactly when I am thirsty or tired or in need of a sympathetic ear. It can't be possible, but yet it is. And every day I wonder about my own selfish habits and expectations: do I witness the needs of others? Can I learn to focus in a better way?

Arrivals and departures

We'll begin our travels where many others do – at the airport. One flight takes off every evening from Kennedy Airport to Casablanca, and the flight crew of Royal Air Maroc welcomes a diverse population of travellers: some to explore business ventures in a progressive North African nation, others for a grand adventure.

I don't know all of these stories, but the ones I like best are about reunions: immigrants heading home for the first time, perhaps the only time. Day after day, these flights include people who are going home, finally, after many years of longing for their loved ones. They may have made homes for themselves in the United States, but they have left important pieces of themselves in their homeland.

Sometimes memories are evoked only in context, and so the immigrant feels a need to return for these memories, to gather them up and hold them. There are touchstones in Morocco that they must touch again.

As they return home, they may have someone special to introduce, someone who has never been to Morocco before. This may be a spouse, a partner, a friend, perhaps even children who have never seen this other home of theirs, who have never met loved ones who pray daily for them, who yearn to meet them. And the travellers feel assured that they will be warmly welcomed, assured that the Moroccan way is hospitality and kindness. This is a certainty for those who return home, no matter how many years they have been away.

And so, as the travellers fill their suitcases with gifts and wait to board their flights, their families in Morocco prepare sumptuous meals and ride long miles to the airport. On both sides of the Atlantic, the families anticipate their reunion with great joy, harbouring any secret hopes and anxieties quietly within them.

At the airport, we see a family of five preparing to board our flight. This is a family that moves us; it is a family that would move almost any human heart. They are so clearly loving, tender, and sweet, that their distant relatives will soon be overwhelmed by emotion at seeing them together. Is it possible there is not a hint of discord in this family? They exude a lovely perfection, an harmonious aspect. For us, a view of this family provides a moment of hope, and also a hint of jealousy and cynicism.

Even as I see them, I begin to invent a story about them. They will remain for me a creation, a fiction, a story. Of course I know a few people who resemble them, whose lives move in harmony and peace, and if you are lucky you might recognise your own spirit in Susan's gentleness, Daoud's thoughtfulness, or the happiness of their children.

Are they living the life that others only dream of? Or do they have their difficult moments, too? Imagine how it is for them – this trip is expensive. Imagine the sacrifices they make so that they can travel sometimes to their family. Maybe they can't do it every year, and maybe the children grow up without knowing their grandparents, without being able to communicate in a language that remains unfamiliar to them. And when they travel, they carry many hopes and expectations that can't possibly be met in the short time allowed. Yet everyone will try, and as these five people make their way to Fez, dozens of people in Morocco are working at full speed to prepare for their visit – making food, cleaning house, telling everyone in the neighbourhood about the progress of the travellers, inviting one another to stop by, of course, and then thinking of all the food that must be prepared, not only for the travellers but for the neighbours and family who will accompany them wherever they go.

There's a young woman watching them. At first I think she is writing in her journal like me, but then I realise she is sketching. Perhaps she is trying to capture the spirit of this family, too. I wonder about her, where she's going, why she seems to be travelling alone. Is she an artist hoping to find new material for her work? Is she meeting a friend overseas? Or a stranger? Does she understand all the unspoken rules of the place where she is going? She looks a bit nervous.

I wonder what I looked like, the first time I went to Morocco. I was probably like her, not drawing, but taking notes in the airport. I was also nervous and wondering whether I was going to be able to do the work I had promised to do, my first field study on my own. I was studying Moroccan Arabic then, so different from the Modern Standard Arabic I had learned in university. I hadn't even begun to study Tamazight – that would come much later. I had some contacts, some friends of friends, all very tenuous. I had moments of fear, of insecurity, some doubts and regrets, but mostly, I felt successful, and the work I did then is still my ongoing work. And there I met my beloved, through friends of friends of friends. He was doing similar work, and he invited me to join him in the Middle Atlas, to see the festivals that I was so curious about. He told me secretly that he wanted to make some things transparent – sex tourism, secret prisons, political movements – he wanted to unravel some of the mysteries.

As a native of the country, native speaker of the languages, his anthropology is more nuanced, and he has more access than most. I found myself falling in love with him, and he with me. And now I can turn and smile at him, and he'll know what I'm thinking about. He'll know I'm already inventing silly stories about the people around us, stories I'll whisper to him on the flight.

Going home

Once on board their flight, Susan and Daoud arrange the children behind them. Salma, of course, sits between her younger brothers, Adel and Isaac. The role of mediator is one she takes on willingly, not only because she loves them but also because she enjoys it – as the older sister of two boys she is both nurturing and authoritative. Daoud sits in the aisle seat in front of Isaac so that no one else must endure his restless feet. When Elizabeth boards, a few minutes later, her window seat is next to Susan.

As the plane soars over the Atlantic, Susan rests her head against her husband's shoulder. He turns a bit to adjust his body to hers, reaching his arm around her and kissing the top of her head. Susan leans forward to touch the screen so they can see the map together. Just seven hours between New York and Casablanca. Soon they will sleep again in Fez, waking to the smells and sounds of home.

Much later, when the pilot announces that the passengers can move freely about the cabin, Susan squeezes Daoud's hand and unfastens her seatbelt. She wants to stand up to see the children, walk around a bit to relieve the tension in her body. She turns back towards her children. The boys are restful with their books. She asks Salma with a smile: "Doing well?" Salma is her oldest child, her only daughter, a girl now becoming grown, changing daily, sometimes her friend and sometimes a confusion of nerves and edges. Salma replies with a smile.

"Soon you will see your grandmother again," Susan whispers. Salma nods, her eyes bright in anticipation of all that is still before her.

Salma hasn't seen her grandmother, her aunt Amal, her many cousins, since she was twelve years old. Now, at fifteen, she is a different person, a bit less confident. She wonders whether she has been loved or forgotten. If she knew how they pray for her, every day five times, how her name is evoked in their daily conversations – if she knew how often they think of her, how they kiss her picture each day, she would never doubt, but this is Salma, always wondering.

When Susan returns to her seat, Elizabeth shifts slightly to create space. "Thank you," Susan says, and Elizabeth nods. "Are you staying in Morocco?" Susan asks her, "Or transferring to another flight in Casablanca?"

"I'm staying in Morocco, in Essouaira," Elizabeth replies.

"What a beautiful city! You must be excited."

"Yes, I am, of course," says Elizabeth. "Have you been to Essouaira?"

"Only once, many years ago. It's very nice – relaxing, near the sea. You will love it. Is this your first trip to Morocco?"

"Yes. I'm a bit nervous," Elizabeth confesses.

"Are you travelling alone?"

"Yes. No. I have a friend."

"Don't worry. My first trip to Morocco was almost twenty years ago, when I joined the Peace Corps after college. I was so nervous then, and excited too. I didn't know what to expect, and my Arabic was terrible. Do you speak Arabic? Or French?"

"French, yes, my father is Québécois," Elizabeth explains.

"French will help you quite a bit. I had some Modern Standard Arabic courses in college, which aren't as helpful as you might think because Moroccan Arabic is quite different. We had Moroccan Arabic classes in Peace Corps, but it took me a while to learn. I used my college French until I could manage the local languages."

Elizabeth has been chatting with Mahmoud online for over a year, and yet she has never told him that she is fluent in French. At first it was because that part of her childhood, the French-speaking part, remains painful in her memory, and she prefers to use English. But now she has confessed her life to Mahmoud, and he knows all about her parents, her childhood, her feelings about her life, her thoughts about the future. He knows that she wants to develop as an artist, and his enthusiasm for her art is what most attracts her.

She feels a little guilty, as if her French is a secret, and she concedes a self-protective motive for not telling him. She knows that French might serve her well if she needs a secret weapon or mode of escape. This is a man who has become her most intimate confidant, and yet they have never met. She feels justified in holding back this one thing, just for now.

"I'm sorry. I must be keeping you from your book," Susan says.

But Elizabeth isn't ready to sit quietly alone. She feels scared, terrified. "No, it's fine."

"What are you reading?" Susan ventures, now becoming curious about Elizabeth, her solitude. Why is this young woman travelling alone?

"*In Morocco*. I know it is terribly outdated."

"Edith Wharton?" Susan smiles, remembering. "My grandmother dusted off her copy for me when I received my Peace Corps assignment. Isn't that funny?"

"I was reading travel guides, but they scared me. I almost cancelled the trip."

"Wharton may be outdated, but I appreciate her ambiguity. In some ways she is more accurate than any current travel writer, and she sets the right mood. History moves quickly in some ways and slowly in others. You'll see."

"Thank you."

"Well, I love Morocco very much, and I like Wharton's impression, even if it is a little idealistic. Sometimes I get frustrated with her because she pretends to be the only 'westerner' in Morocco, and then she follows with a chapter about meeting Europeans and attending their parties. It's whatever she wants at the moment, I guess. And if I'm going to be really honest, I've felt the same way at times, as if I'm the only American in Morocco. Believe me, that's a momentary feeling because I'll run into some tourists around the next corner. Anyway, foreigners can't seem to write well about Morocco. Maybe it isn't possible. And the movies are even worse. The night before I left for Morocco, my little sister made me watch Casablanca with her. I was really upset! My sister imagined me in smoky nightclubs with a silky dress. I wanted her to be more serious. More like Wharton maybe."

Elizabeth smiles politely, but Susan realises she is talking too much. She wants to engage Elizabeth in conversation because she is curious, and a little concerned. Because of her job, she knows of many young women who have got themselves into trouble abroad. She knows of unscrupulous men who lure women with offers of love and happiness, who are smitten by the idea of American citizenship, their fantasies of wealth and promise. Susan is suspicious and cynical sometimes, and she feels nervous about the safety of this woman beside her.

"Excuse me, I didn't catch your name."

"Sorry. Elizabeth."

"Elizabeth, I'm Susan. Please don't think I'm nosy, but is someone meeting you at the airport?"

"Yes, my friend. I mean my boyfriend."

"I'm very glad to hear that. Travelling alone here can be dangerous. Some of the guys here will do anything for an American passport." Susan laughs, aiming for levity, but it doesn't work. Elizabeth shifts uncomfortably; she seems offended by Susan's remark.

Elizabeth has waited months for this moment: to be aboard an airplane to Casablanca, to see what her fate will bring. To her credit, Elizabeth is more reserved than she admits to others. She may seem utterly reckless to an outsider, but inside she is self-protective and sceptical, too. Her hope is that Mahmoud is all he claims to be, but she knows everyone has a shiny face to present to the world and a dark side to keep hidden. This is why she must travel to meet him: she must look more deeply within. She must know the man who claims to love her and discover whether she loves him too.

Now Daoud pokes Susan with his elbow. His gentle way of reminding her to mind her own business.

But Susan can't help herself: "Where did you meet your boyfriend?"

Elizabeth drops her eyes and shifts back in her seat. "I haven't actually met him yet. We've been chatting online for a while."

"Well! Hmm. That's exciting." Now Susan pokes back at Daoud. Her way of saying that she cannot be silent. Elizabeth concerns her.

Susan works to keep any note of condescension from creeping into her voice. She decides to tell her own story, a true one: "I met my husband in Morocco. When I first saw him, I was very attracted to him. The Peace Corps hired him to train us in Moroccan Arabic, so he was my teacher for eight weeks. I was lucky to have a chance to really get to know him before we became involved with each other. I could see how he treated other people, and I could see his work ethic. I met his family when we were friends, before we admitted that we loved each other." Susan is lecturing now. She regrets her tone of voice a little, but she keeps going, punching key words for emphasis.

"We became friends quite slowly, in fact. Daoud never intended to marry an American. He resisted the idea for a while because he never wanted to be separated from his family. I'm trying to tell you, Elizabeth, and I'm sorry if you think that I'm interfering, but you have to be careful not to rush into anything, especially overseas."

Elizabeth has heard a similar speech before. Just yesterday, when Elizabeth brought the last of her belongings to store in her mother's basement. Her mother, hysterical with grief and fear, shrieked similar warnings and threats at Elizabeth's impassive facade. Now, as Elizabeth hears Susan's voice droning on, her chief concern is how to make it go away. She tries this: "Well, when you meet the right person…"

Susan takes a deep breath of resolve. She is compelled to say something important and useful to Elizabeth, to offer a safe haven, to save her life. Ignoring her husband's persistent jabs, she interrupts, "Maybe, but even the person who seems right can be very wrong. Sometimes you misjudge a person, and there are severe consequences. I'm just saying that a relationship is a big commitment, and you have to act cautiously, consider every angle. I don't know you at all, and we just met, but sometimes a stranger can tell you the truth better than a friend."

Susan may be guided by empathy, but empathy doesn't always lead her to such intrusive methods.

Empathy usually means bringing a casserole to an elderly neighbour or being the first to visit a sick relative. Susan tries not to offer advice unless explicitly asked, and yet today she sits beside Elizabeth and gives this unwelcome lecture. Why this compulsion to advise Elizabeth? Susan asks herself this question. Very likely it is not simply Elizabeth, but rather a symbol that Elizabeth represents: the vulnerable young woman, the one you want to shake some sense into. Susan feels helpless now, too, imagining Elizabeth alone and suffering, completely lost in a foreign country, depending for her life on a man who could be a predator. Or perhaps not a predator, but rather a man who is seduced by Hollywood visions of the American dream. Perhaps what brings them together doesn't matter; perhaps they come to love one another over time.

He could also be a wonderful person who is sincerely in love with Elizabeth. Susan could be doing damage to a man who doesn't deserve it.

There is something about Elizabeth that moves Susan. Perhaps she sees something of herself in Elizabeth – a young and naïve girl, off on an exciting adventure with too little fear and too many dangers.

Elizabeth looks away towards the window. Some people, she thinks, like nothing better than to interfere with the happiness of others. "Listen Susan, I appreciate your concern, but it really isn't necessary." Elizabeth looks again at the clear blue sky, wishing for an air pocket to send the plane into a dip, anything to redirect Susan's attention away from her.

"Elizabeth, I'll leave you to your book, but please listen to me. We're going to be here for two weeks, in Fez. If you are here beyond our stay, you can also call my husband's family for anything you need. My sister-in-law speaks English and French very well. You never know what might happen. Sometimes these things work out, and other times, well, I'm sorry to intrude, but I remember my first days abroad, first as a student overseas and later as a new Peace Corps volunteer, and it can be disconcerting. Please, call this number if you need anything at all."

Elizabeth controls an urge to roll her eyes as she reaches for the proffered slip of paper. "This really isn't necessary, Susan. I appreciate your help, but my boyfriend is capable of handling things in his own country."

"I'm sure you are right. I hope you enjoy your time here and see a lot of interesting sites. Morocco is a beautiful country. Have a wonderful time, Elizabeth. I hope everything works out well for you."

"Thank you." Elizabeth feels bewildered and lonely as Susan turns back to her husband. She won't throw the number away. The truth is that it gives her a sense of comfort. She tucks the number inside her book where her finger has been holding her place. She has lost interest in reading. She leans back against the seat and looks out of the window. After a moment, she reaches forward to push the button on the map in front of her. She can see the little airplane crossing the Atlantic Ocean, far to the north of New York and Morocco. In a few hours, she will meet her Mahmoud and set her fears to rest.

As they disembark, Daoud reaches for Susan's heaviest bag. He grins, his voice low, "Did you save her?" His tone is light as he jokes with her, but she knows that his question is in earnest.

"Probably not."

"Maybe she thought you were a secret agent."

Susan smiles at this: "She would be right, but why would a secret agent care about Elizabeth? She's not a threat to national security, only to herself."

"Working for the agency doesn't make you a superhero, Susan. I'm sorry to break this news to you."

Susan laughs now, too, her thoughts turning inward, to family and home. "What do you think your mother will cook for us?"

"Your favourite, first, then mine tomorrow. She's probably supervising the butcher at this very minute, to assure the lamb is perfect. Listen, Suzy, are you sure you agree with my plan for my mother? You don't mind?"

"I do, dear heart. I'm not jealous at all."

"It's important, Susan. She's getting older, and this may be her only chance. We are expected to make this trip, each of us, and I'm the only one who can take her. I promise that you and I will go together when the children are older. Please understand."

"I do understand, Daoud, truly."

As they walk towards the gates to meet Amal and the cousins who have come to the airport, Susan and Daoud stop for a moment to watch Elizabeth walk uncertainly towards the crowd. There are several young men who could be there to meet her, standing awkwardly, some with placards of welcome, some with flowers. There are a few other women like Elizabeth, too, walking towards their fate in unaccustomed movements. They watch Elizabeth as she is approached a few times, as she shakes her head, until she finally meets her beloved: a small man, dishevelled, as if he had slept all night on a bus. He smiles, happy to see her, and she smiles, too. They embrace, and he kisses her, full on the lips, in a manner more often seen in Hollywood movies than in Moroccan public places.

"Bold move," whispers Daoud to Susan, and Susan nods.

"Seems like he's done this before. He needs a shower, and an iron."

Daoud laughs. And then it is too late to think of Elizabeth, as Susan, Daoud, and the children are swept into an embracing crowd of relatives, with shouts of joy, exclamations, and appraisals.

Susan's fears for Elizabeth are not unfounded. Her work for the agency brings her into the private lives of many people like Elizabeth and Mahmoud. If you had told Susan in college that her studies of the Middle East and North Africa would make her uniquely qualified to conduct surveillance of American citizens and their mostly innocent friends abroad, she would have given you a lecture on the Bill of Rights, with a special focus on the Fourth Amendment. And yet this has become her work, monitoring websites to seek information on threats to national security.

Most of the websites are populated by innocents, and incidents of interest to the agency are rare. Pathways, for example, is a website that Susan watches. Most of the members are sincere in their purpose, which is to help one another facilitate low-budget travel. The concept is simple: members offer to host one another, sometimes providing guest rooms at their homes, sometimes assisting with low-cost hotels. Hosts might volunteer to provide some meals for the travellers or to show them around the local area; then, at some later date, the traveller plans to reciprocate at home. For the most part, Pathways provides a useful service to travellers and allows members to meet interesting people from around the world. Potential travellers can learn about the places they intend to visit; they can discuss how, when, and where to travel, learn of pitfalls and recommendations.

The agency keeps a close eye on chatrooms like this – these boring and predictable streams of chatter – to monitor for dangerous characters. Most discussions are in English, though many occur in other languages. Because it is online, languages that don't use the Latin alphabet have had to invent spellings that do, so Susan has become adept at following the development of languages as they adapt to the demands of online communication. Foreign words don't alarm Susan, of course, who is an accomplished linguist with a team of experts to draw upon.

Susan is alert to two types of personalities in particular: the domineering and the ingratiating. A dominant personality can somehow compel a weaker-minded person to do something daring or unusual. An ingratiating personality can do the same, using the illusion of weakness to compel people. In either case, otherwise innocent people can be drawn into dangerous scenarios.

Yet there is humour in Susan's daily work. Most of her time is spent reading banal flirtations between timid or awkward people. And because the chat patterns are fairly predictable, it is easy for Susan to recognise unusual behaviour. Sometimes Susan regrets that she is not paid to save individuals from themselves; there is nothing that Susan can do to help a consenting adult in a foolish situation. Yet she often fears for the safety of travellers, especially women planning to travel alone, like Elizabeth, to countries where they have scant resources and little understanding of cultural norms.

What might alert Susan would be a request for one traveller to transport or deliver an object overseas, or signs that a person is laundering money or messages. If she notices suspicious chatter, she orders an investigation. Susan has been commended several times for foiling nefarious plots, and she is often recognised at the agency for her keen and discriminating eye. Her colleagues know that she isn't likely to raise a false alarm: they take her recommendations quite seriously. She doesn't waste people's time, and she knows her limits. Still, her sympathy is often aroused by an innocent person she would like very much to save.

Many of the travellers are not careful on the websites, and they share too much. Susan sometimes shakes her head in disgust as she watches women sharing their secrets and desires online. She sees their unmet emotional needs scrolling across the screen. Sometimes Susan imagines herself reaching out across the space that separates her from one of these women, grabbing her by the shoulders and shaking. She wants somehow to reach them with warnings and admonitions. She wants them to realise that certain predators are only interested in their citizenship and its many rewards. She wants them to guard their properties and their emotions from men who would take them on roller-coaster rides of marriage, immigration, divorce, and financial ruin.

At home Susan shares her thoughts with Daoud, the only person whom she confides in. Sometimes she can see a disaster in process, and she wishes she could do something to help.

"Remember, Suzy, you fell for a charming foreigner, too." Daoud is always sensitive to how Americans perceive him and his marriage to Susan, but Susan doesn't think of this.

"There's so little I can do for them, Daoud. I just sit and watch, helpless."

"Suzy, you can't save them from themselves, and they wouldn't thank you for your heroic efforts. Your job is to protect the pursuit of happiness, not happiness itself."

Elizabeth travels alone

heArtblog, Sept 12

Dear friends and family – first of all, thank you to everyone for your well-wishes and kind thoughts as I embark on this potentially life-changing journey. Yes, I bought a round-trip ticket – some of you thought I wouldn't – but we'll see if I actually use the return. I'm so smitten at the moment that I feel I could stay in Morocco forever.

I met a lovely family on the flight. They were so joyful and happy to be visiting their loved ones in Morocco. They represent everything I've ever wanted in my life – true love, sweet and beautiful children – I mean, true happiness! The way they laugh together – it's all too sweet for words.

Consider Elizabeth for a moment: this is a woman to feel for. She is sweet, kind, shy, and vulnerable. Her trip to Morocco has the potential for total disaster, and there are a great number of people who feel that they know better and would like very much to reason with her. But let's allow Elizabeth to follow her own path, and we will see whether the journey is worthwhile for her. Elizabeth has been floating a bit lately, and it might seem prudent to pull her back to earth, but such heroics are impossible with a woman like Elizabeth, whose heart is set on a goal. The only thing to do is to stay close and vigilant – prepare to assist in only the direst of emergencies. Elizabeth may not know exactly how to engage with the world, and yet engagement is all she desires.

The world is strange to Elizabeth; she has always tended towards small spaces where she feels safe, but not at the moment; she is poised now to take a large chunk out of life and see what it feels like. She will make some mistakes, of course, but she will be changed irrevocably as well, and she is ready for a change.

The promise of love has called to her, and Elizabeth has decided upon yes. She says no so often – to her whims and fantasies, to her parents' demands, to her artistic talents, to the melodies and rhythms within her. This time she has chosen yes, and she is moving in a new way.

We can have some faith in Elizabeth; her heart is good and pure, and her spirit is stronger than it seems. She is out of practice because she has been sequestering herself for these several years, since she gave up on her dream of creating great works of art and settled for more steady work in graphic design. She is about to put a challenge to herself, and we have a close view on her movements. We can only wish her the best and then stand back to watch how it goes for her.

And yet, while Elizabeth hopes for true love and all its trappings, she does remain sceptical. This is why she buys the return ticket that she may or may not use. This is what keeps her awake at night, long past the darkness and into the dawn. There is a dark and cynical side to Elizabeth that causes her to question not only Mahmoud's intentions but also her own. She remembers when her own family seemed happy together, how abruptly it all ended, how bewildered she felt as a child, and how betrayed she still feels.

Elizabeth is confused and heady, unaccustomed to being a man's object of desire, impatient to be touched affectionately and adored. If you, like many others, are wondering what has infected Elizabeth, the answer is simply this: the promise of adoration has caused her to gamble her meagre savings on a plane ticket, stuff her bra and socks with enough cash to sustain herself for two weeks, and fly off to Casablanca. Since this trip is a hasty and unusual risk for Elizabeth, she has not attempted to explain it to anyone; instead, she maintains a confident manner in defence of her decision while inside she suffers immense anxiety.

What Elizabeth hopes for, more than anything, is to throw that return ticket away. She hopes to stay in Morocco until she has proven to herself and the world the greatness of Mahmoud and the strength of his love. Only after they have married and lived along the North African shores for many years will she return in triumph.

Elizabeth wants a dramatic romance followed by a secure and lasting commitment. She feels, dormant within her, a grand capacity for love, and today it is awakened by the enormity of her decision. When she boards the plane, she is thinking of her last conversation with Mahmoud. He had told her of his belief in love at first sight and how he expected them to feel it upon their first meeting. He had expressed his hope that he might someday tell their grandchildren of their fateful first encounter.

Elizabeth doesn't believe in love at first sight, but she is glad that Mahmoud does. She likes his optimism; she hopes it provides a ballast for her weakness. And while she may not believe in love at first sight, she does know the power of first impressions. She hopes to use their first moments wisely: she wants Mahmoud to appreciate the gravity of her decision to accept his invitation.

Does Elizabeth have a chance? Not with Mahmoud, unfortunately. As your narrator, I share Susan's doubts, and I, also, would like to free Elizabeth from the maelstrom of Mahmoud's inner chaos. There is a complicated road ahead for Elizabeth. You may believe that I am quite misguided regarding her, or too pessimistic a narrator. You may believe that Susan's fears are overly wrought. Perhaps we don't fully account for Elizabeth's desperate need to feel loved. The reality is, whenever a catastrophe approaches, there is very little that can be done to stop it. Another reality to face is this: Elizabeth's path may be tangled and gnarled and sharp with thorns, but it is fully hers, and she wouldn't trade it for any rose-scented and manicured garden, at least not yet.

Mahmoud is not a threat to national security, only to the well-being of a few unlucky women. His chats would never alert Susan, although his chat partners might arouse her sympathy. When Mahmoud chats, he adopts the first name of his favourite theorist, Edward Said. As Edward, his words are affected, crafted to impress and charm his chat partners. Once he knows enough about the other person, he drops hints to suggest they have much in common. Not only with Elizabeth: Mahmoud maintains various conversations with dexterity, and insincerity, often copying words from one chat to paste in another. If his conversations lack coherence, his partners are forgiving. They understand that English is neither his first nor his second language, and they marvel at his lovely words.

Mahmoud's gyrations would tire most people, and indeed it is somewhat exhausting to be Mahmoud, a person so driven by his elusive dream that he cannot relax for a moment: but then again his dream is a source of energy that serves him. Mahmoud is scrappy, and like all scrappy people, he never relents. It is as if someone is always chasing him, and he must be always on the run. What does he run from? From himself, perhaps, from his guilt. In every man is the side he would present to his own mother and the side he hides in shame. In a man like Mahmoud: greedy, covetous, insatiable in his ambition, one side runs in disgust from the other, and the result is a dog chasing his tail.

Can you blame Mahmoud? He simply wants what everyone else wants: a love so great as to lift him to a promised land. But Samir considers his friend's plan ridiculous. He has heard all of Mahmoud's crazy ideas, and he does not support such nonsense.

Samir knows all about the immigrant life from his uncle in Toronto, whom he visits on occasion. His uncle can hardly afford their small apartment full of people. His wife works long days, too, and her pay is meagre. At night, Samir can hear mice coming and going, and he can hardly sleep for fear of a rodent or roach crawling over his body at night. The city, to Samir, is a cold crush of foreign bodes and foreign smells. After a few days in Toronto, Samir longs for Morocco, where his mother has servants to care for his food and clothing. In Toronto there is no time for family conversation or prayers. He never hears a muezzin, and he doesn't remember to pray on time, so he tries to compensate in the mornings or before he sleeps. In Toronto, he feels guilty burdening his overworked aunt with extra chores, but he adds his laundry to the pile nevertheless. The worst of it all is that he doesn't trust the food. The family eats meat from the grocery, uncertain of the source or the butcher. When his aunt is too tired to cook, Samir goes with his cousins to eat unsatisfying junk food.

Just last month Mahmoud had hinted to Samir, "Hey friend! Elizabeth will come next month – don't forget!" and this irritated Samir.

"Why mustn't I forget, Mahmoud? Why should I care what visitors you have?"

"Because she needs a place. I'm going to need your help, brother."

"I'm not your brother, Mahmoud! It's not my fault you have only sisters! Look, Kristy was just here for you, and already you've thrown her aside. Last year it was that French girl – what was her name? You probably don't even remember."

"Simone?"

"Simone. Yes. And Kristy. And how many others? So now you intend to break Elizabeth's heart as well. No, Mahmoud, I won't host another woman for you, and I suggest you become more serious about your future. You'll never make anything of yourself on the back of a woman."

"You don't understand, Samir!"

"What's to understand about you, Mahmoud? That you want to go to New York? Then go! Apply to Columbia and Harvard. Get accepted. Wait for your visa, like everyone else."

"Impossible, Samir."

"Impossible? You may be right. American universities are expensive, and you are only going to be mopping floors if you go to New York, even if your poetry is good. But please explain to me how a woman changes the scenario. I just can't see it. Or better yet, Mahmoud, stop being foolish! Go to Ibn Zohr or Mohammed V. The comparative literature programmes are excellent, as good as any programmes abroad. Study, become a professor, and use that leverage to move away from here if you still want to. Arabic is popular over there now. Abdellatif got a job teaching Arabic, but he did it on his own, not because of a woman. Make a plan that doesn't depend on a woman!"

Samir does not understand the feverish desires of the immigrant, and he does not sympathise with Mahmoud's perspective at all. He feels certain Mahmoud's life in Morocco would be quite satisfying if only Mahmoud learned to practise gratitude and humility. He has tired of Mahmoud gnawing on about his dream of living in New York and meeting Homi Bhabha in his office at Harvard.

Samir has hosted several of Mahmoud's international visitors already, and he has tired of Mahmoud's requests for food and housing for these women. This is why Samir enlists his beloved, Sanaa, in a devious plan. When Elizabeth calls Mahmoud, preparing for her trip to Morocco, Sanaa pretends to be interested in welcoming her and encouraging her visit. She walks away from Samir and Mahmoud to warn Elizabeth of Mahmoud's unsavoury motives. In the meantime, Samir tries to rescue Elizabeth by discouraging Mahmoud: "Mahmoud, listen to me," he says, "Forget her! Marry a nice girl from home. These Americans are jealous and unreasonable. They don't love harmony at home; they don't care about it. They care too much about autonomy; any sacrifice is demeaning to them. Think about it, Mahmoud! Try again for Zahra. She will graduate soon with a master's degree. Her parents like you. Well, maybe they do, but they like your parents at least."

As she talks with Elizabeth, Sanaa wanders away from the two friends. She is weaving among crowds of children walking and bicycling home from school. She is nearly sideswiped by one bicyclist struggling to control his vehicle with a passenger on his handlebars. She tries earnestly to convince Elizabeth of Mahmoud's selfishness without causing unnecessary pain: "I've known Mahmoud all his life, Elizabeth, and I still don't understand him. He has never been kind to women. He seems to hate us. He treats women as lesser creatures and glorifies his male friends. Even so, he has been infatuated with my friend, Zahra, for many years, but she despises him. I have seen him trying to court a few other women lately, but he isn't nice to them, and they quickly lose interest."

"Am I a fool?" Elizabeth asks Sanaa, "Am I just a stupid fool? Is that what you are trying to tell me?"

Now Elizabeth seems on the threshold of tears, and Sanaa considers her next words carefully. She wants to shout Yes! You are an utter fool to waste your money on a single phone call to Mahmoud, but she takes a kinder approach. "It is easy to fall in love, Elizabeth, but it is never easy to determine whether the person loves you back."

Sanaa is always nervous to express herself in English, especially on the phone where she can't see the other person's facial expressions and gestures, but she manages as best she can. She wants to convince Elizabeth of two things: that she, Sanaa, does not act in self-interest, and that he, Mahmoud, most definitely does. Elizabeth, surprised by Sanaa's interest in her, feels grateful at first for an opportunity to talk with someone who knows Mahmoud well. She feels curious about Mahmoud and some of the inconsistencies she has noticed in his stories. But as she listens to Sanaa, she realises that Sanaa may not be a reliable source for information; rather, Sanaa seems bent on destroying Mahmoud's character, and Elizabeth despairs of learning anything. She listens politely, wondering about Sanaa's motives: perhaps Sanaa wants Mahmoud for herself; perhaps she is a disloyal friend.

Sanaa's message might have caught hold several months earlier, but not at this time. Sanaa has arrived too late. Elizabeth has made too many sacrifices for Mahmoud already, and she has a plane ticket to visit him. Even though Elizabeth has long harboured some doubts of her own, she does not want to believe Sanaa's intentions to be pure. As soon as Sanaa passes the phone back to Mahmoud, Elizabeth tattles to him. By the expressions on Mahmoud's face, Sanaa can see that Elizabeth has betrayed her, and Sanaa feels disgusted. She has tried to establish solidarity, to be helpful to a woman in trouble, and this is the thanks that she gets. She motions to Samir, who is shaking his head, annoyed, and they leave without saying goodbye.

By revealing Sanaa, Elizabeth has proven her devotion to Mahmoud, and his response is gratifying. He tells her how he values her confidence in him, how lucky he is to have such an honest woman, how his love has grown incrementally by her action. Later in the day Mahmoud attacks Sanaa by posting unkind and cruel lies about her online – comments that create a fury in their circle of friends until Samir's threats frighten Mahmoud sufficiently for him to delete them. After this, Sanaa and Mahmoud never greet one another, although Mahmoud continues to ingratiate himself to Samir. Above all, Mahmoud realises the value of male companions, and he refuses to allow any woman to interfere in his friendships.

Samir and Sanaa have no regrets. They feel sorry for Elizabeth, and they wish she would understand that her lover is making her foolish.

Susan, secret agent

February 24, 1980

I'm 12 years old today. Walter Cronkite announced 112 days last night, so I asked my parents for a special birthday. We are going to try, all day, not to use any electricity. We won't have any hot water, and we'll eat our dinner by candlelight. Dad even set up the grill outside, even though it's going to be really cold. President Carter asked us to conserve more energy because it will help the hostages. I know my family can do better, and not just on my birthday. What I really want for my birthday is solar panels for our house, like our president installed at the White House. If we really want peace in the Middle East, we are going to have to make some changes.

When Iranian students and militants, acting in defiance of American imperialism, overtake the United States Embassy in 1979, Susan's career begins. She is only eleven years old, yet the Iranian hostage crisis is formative for her. Her parents are surprised to see their young daughter reading newspapers so that she can learn about every detail of the 444-day ordeal.

Susan follows with rapt attention as President Carter's administration works to negotiate the release of the hostages. She listens carefully each night as Walter Cronkite opens his nightly news broadcast with the report of how many days the hostages have been held and what progress has been made to release them.

Her careful attention to this episode in world history results in Susan becoming familiar with differing perspectives on her own country. Where she had once felt at ease in her small, safe community in upstate New York, she comes to realise the influence and power of the United States and the many tensions its prevailing power creates around the world. When the Ayatollah Khomeini complains that the United States took the entire nation of Iran hostage in 1953, Susan looks back to the events of history, and she comes to understand that Carter's public toast to the shah, his audacity to presume to speak for the people of Iran by declaring the shah a beloved leader, may have precipitated the crisis unnecessarily.

Susan's innovative educational process, based not at school but in her own study of the Iranian hostage crisis, expands to include a revised understanding of American history. One day, the militants say that they will release the African American and female hostages, saying that these hostages are already victims, have already suffered enough due to American racism and sexism. This fact does not receive much attention in the American press, but it catches Susan's eye, and she asks many questions of her teachers and parents regarding the decision. When their answers are not satisfying, she goes to the library to investigate further. Answers are not readily apparent to her, and with her limited reading ability as a child, she cannot seem to uncover what she needs. When she receives only tepid responses to her questions, she wishes she could ask the questions abroad, wondering whether people in other countries might provide more frank and comprehensive answers than the adults of her own community are willing to offer. She becomes increasingly annoyed that the university students in Iran know more about her own country than she does.

Susan is torn between conflicting opinions: are the hostages being treated like guests, as the militants claim? It seems unlikely to her, and she stays awake at night, fearing for their safety and imagining all sorts of variations on the themes of the crisis. She wonders about her president, a man she considers kind-hearted and for whom her parents had enthusiastically voted. Is he at fault? Is he doing all the right things to assure a successful result? Why does he endure petty insults from the Ayatollah? What do his wife and mother say to him behind closed doors? Why is the shah allowed to travel freely to the United States for medical care while the hostages continue their suffering?

Then the helicopters of Operation Eagle Claw fail, and Susan wonders again: why aren't they checked over carefully for mechanical problems before attempting such an important mission? She feels there is much that is unfair, peculiar, and poorly explained for children.

The ultimate humiliation, of course, comes on January 20th, 1981, when the hostages are finally released, just minutes after President Carter becomes former president Carter. On this day, Susan runs home from school to see the newspaper. Half of the front page is dedicated to President Reagan's inauguration, and the other half to the release of the hostages. Susan's parents understand her indignant response; by now, they too have been drawn into their daughter's obsession. Furious to see Reagan taking credit for the peaceful release of the hostages, Susan sulks about it for weeks, and her commitment to a future career in foreign service is firmly resolved.

While the hostage crisis creates an atmosphere of demonstrative patriotism and anti-Islamic fervour in the United States, for Susan it has a different effect. She feels there are misunderstandings between nations that must be exposed and ameliorated. She knows, even as a child, that her life will be dedicated to this project. This goal becomes her guiding light and undying passion. Susan, now fascinated by the politics of the Middle East, continues to study all she can about the relationships between nations and the root causes of their conflicts. Beginning with the Iraqi invasion of Iran, and the Soviet Union's invasion of Afghanistan, she creates an archive of news clippings. Her mother helps her to develop a system of files so that she can organise her materials. This intensive study of the Middle East develops with every essay she writes in high school, always centring her focus on some new aspect in her desire for world peace. She considers every angle, from religion, literature, history, politics, geography, and economics. Her teachers fully expect her to win the Nobel Peace Prize one day, and they become dedicated to supporting her interests.

With such an intense focus on her future, Susan has no trouble getting accepted into top universities for political science; she decides upon Georgetown University, wanting to be close to the pulse of her nation's political energies.

While her classmates at Georgetown dither about selecting a major in their first two years of studies, Susan sets out immediately on the path she had long imagined. In her first semester, she enrols in advanced French, beginning Arabic, comparative politics, and international relations. She doesn't bother with course numbers, enrolling heedlessly in classes meant for upper-class students.

When it comes to selecting a study abroad programme, Susan easily decides upon Amman, Jordan, dutifully studying while her friends revel in Paris, Florence, and Berlin, stopping only briefly from their festivities to host their parents. But Susan asks her parents to stay home. She can't spend a week speaking English in Jordan when she needs to stay immersed in Arabic. So while the other parents are visiting their children in Europe, Susan's parents go off, somewhat guiltily, to Cancún. "Susan is too focused on her studies to host us," they explain to anyone who asks.

Finally, at her college graduation, Susan announces that she has been accepted to the Peace Corps and assigned to Morocco. Within weeks, she has packed her bags for a two-year commitment.

The night before Susan leaves for her Peace Corps assignment, the family gathers to say goodbye. Her parents have found recipes for Moroccan food, and though they can't tell for certain whether they have replicated a traditional meal, the food is delicious. Her sister has rented *Casablanca* to watch after dinner, and Susan's grandmother gives Susan an old copy of Edith Wharton's travelogue, *In Morocco*. The movie unsettles and upsets Susan, not because it has any relevance to the journey ahead of her, but just the opposite. It highlights her family's miscomprehension of her life; they seem to think Susan bears some resemblance to Ingrid Bergman, heading off on a romantic adventure.

June, 1990

I have to say, all their gifts are so thoughtful and sweet, but my grandmother's gift is the one that best suits my feeling at this moment as I set off for Peace Corps. When I applied, I was so excited, but now I'm shaken. That last semester at Georgetown took all my beliefs and basically turned them upside down. I thought Peace Corps would be a chance to help, but my class in post-colonial theory, a literature course that I took at the last minute to fulfil another humanities requirement, well – it has thrown me into a dilemma. These ideas – I had them as a child. I understood them instinctively when I studied the Iran hostage situation so closely. And yet I applied for Peace Corps under the illusion that I would be welcomed by the host nation and that I would do meaningful projects to help the local population. How could it be that a literature course has upset all my ideas, brought me back to reality? Through literature, I can see a truth that other classes have never offered – by showing me the lives of people as they suffer colonisation first hand. By understanding how Africa, Asia, and Latin America were carved up by outside powers, the propping up of certain favoured puppets in critical locations, the enslavement of indigenous populations around the world. I had learned this in theory, but through fiction it becomes real. Sustainable agriculture is cruelly converted into cash cropping, creating an intergenerational cycle of economic dependence, environmental destruction, and manipulation of human labour.

And so, fittingly, it is Edith Wharton - a favourite author of my grandmother's - who best speaks to me at this moment. She creates a world that exists at her convenience, populated in a way that pleases her, and drawn with settings and characters that reassure her. Wharton claims Morocco as her own property: something she has discovered first before any other traveller. But then she betrays herself by introducing a Moroccan town full of Spaniards and Spanish architecture. Then again she moves through a chapter, lonely and desolate, emptied of human contact. Then suddenly robed figures wander mysteriously, and then again a French enclave appears, until just as suddenly the Europeans vanish and Morocco is, again, a land untouched by Europe, Wharton's very own. Then grand Roman ruins, but still Wharton can't admit that the European presence in Morocco has a long history; admitting this would destroy her delusion of exceptionality.

I have learned to deconstruct these arguments, and now I see in Wharton not an innocent young woman abroad but a

tragic colonial attitude: the
deliberate notion that foreign lands
exist to be subjugated. But now I can't
separate myself from Wharton, and I
feel enjoined with her, and now heavy
in spirit.

The sad contrast is that my family,
previously worried and nervous about my
choice of major and study abroad, has
decided to be happy for me and proud
about this journey. They see it as the
fulfilment of my dream. And certainly
it would have been my dream, if only I
hadn't become burdened with information
that shames me. I hold grave
reservations about my decision to
volunteer with the Peace Corps - I
remember so clearly telling my English
professor about my plans - that
expression on her face was devastating.
And yet I haven't planned - in all my
life I haven't - any other options but
to immerse myself in the lives of those
people I thought would welcome my help.

What I have learned too late is that
the reputation of the Peace Corps
around the world is dubious, that
people abroad think of Peace Corps
volunteers as weapons of the CIA, as
perpetuators of colonialism, as
imposters.

And now I am going forward, not allowing
myself to turn back. In Wharton, I

recognise an overt colonial attitude, and I am using it to explore my own motives. Did I expect to be a "different sort" of Peace Corps volunteer? Some sort of revolutionary within? Am I misusing some other country's resources to improve my own resume? Can I do anything worthwhile overseas? Am I serving only myself, or am I part of a nefarious plan? None of these options comforts me.

Susan is moved by their offerings of food, film, and book, but of the three, she prefers her grandmother's gift; it resonates most closely with her conflicted feelings about her journey. This is something she can't share with her family because she doesn't think they will understand, but she feels troubled; she worries that she will do more harm than good for the people of Morocco.

Elizabeth, artist and daughter

heArtblog, Aug 15

"Once upon a time, there was a beautiful princess, named Elizabeth, and her elegant mother, the queen of the land." Every night, I would hurry into my pyjamas, eager for a new instalment of my mother's fantastic stories, always starring Elizabeth, the princess; her mother, the queen; and a full cast of wild and interesting characters.

My mother tells stories as if her life depends upon it, and in some ways I think it does. She would fall apart without her stories to hold her together. Storytelling is my mother's particular talent, and I have always been the principle recipient of these stories (not the only recipient, certainly, as there are many – from random strangers to her closest friends). Throughout my childhood I would find myself, night after night, embarking on uncertain and perilous adventures with my mother at the helm.

Here is a true story that Elizabeth has never been told: Once upon a time, her mother, Sophie, meets the man of her dreams, a tall, handsome man from Quebec whose English is marked with French accents. Sophie herself proposes marriage, and after they marry, she devotes her full attention and energy to satisfying her husband's whims. Is he cold towards her? Not particularly. Is he madly in love? Not ever.

Perhaps there are hints and warnings, but Sophie doesn't notice them. Having been adored throughout her life by her parents, she hasn't any notion of what it means to be unwanted. So accustomed is she to the adoration of others that she scarcely notices her husband's wandering attentions. Then, one day, she delivers the news to her husband that she is pregnant, hoping this will create a stronger bond between them, but it sends him to a fury instead.

Now she hears him on the phone, arguing in French. Perhaps he is discussing pressing matters with his parents; she begins to worry that they don't have enough money for the baby. She fears the unthinkable: a gambling addiction, or worse. But the recipient of his calls is neither his father nor his mother: it is his mistress, also pregnant with a child. And now a wild and turbulent storm, from which the man and two women emerge with a tacit agreement: for the mistress, a provisional loss; for the wife, a fragile victory. Disgraced and dejected, Sophie compromises: she will share him without ever acknowledging it, an arrangement that works for eight years. Then the mistress has a second son, tipping the balance to her side, and Sophie is left alone with a hushed and reticent daughter.

> As a child, reality is a simple thing. I have two parents. I wish I had a sister, but I don't. My mother is always home. Maybe

my father is gone a lot, but they tell me he is working, and I accept that as truth.

At school in Quebec, I feel alone and alienated from the other children, but again, I understand it. My French is basic, and I can't keep up with their banter.

My mother and I have the same day every day, with routines that I like and don't like: morning greetings, breakfast, a lonely day at school without friends, teachers who are pleased with me, an art teacher for whom I am extraordinary. In the evenings, dinner, sometimes with my mother alone, sometimes with both parents, and after homework and dishes, the day's story – a magnificent bedtime story that my mother has been preparing through the day. Sometimes it is only the queen and the princess, but sometimes they are joined by the handsome and valiant king. These heroes go up against vigorous enemies, securing great treasures for the kingdom.

When my parents announce their separation, it is as if one of her evil characters has finally won. A giant ogre or an evil crone has plucked the roof off our house just to see the four walls collapse, and I will never feel safe again. From that day and onward, every day has held within it the potential for utter catastrophe or desolation.

What's probably true is that I've never forgiven my parents for divorcing. Perhaps their divorce was a long and protracted process for them, but for me, it all happened in one abrupt and devastating moment. One day I was an awkward, English-speaking child in Quebec, hardly surviving a French-only school playground, and the next I am adjusting to an even stranger place: my mother's hometown in central New York, where I am teased mercilessly for my Canadian accent. Without the inner confidence to laugh back at them, I retreat into silence. I rarely speak to anyone, my total introversion providing an uncomfortable counterpoint to my mother's gregarious personality. It is in this silence that I become an artist.

Alone with her mother, it is each to her most comforting pattern: Sophie becomes more expressive and outwardly focused, while Elizabeth seeks tight corners and small nests in which to hide. Sophie must entertain; she feels best in front of an adoring audience, and her main focus is Elizabeth, whom she drags out from hiding and puts on display for others to admire.

Sophie can create an audience for herself in any context. In a grocery line, for example, Sophie takes full advantage of the captive audience of waiting customers, capitalising on their boredom for an improvisational monologue: a tragedy about the price of melons or a comedy about her daughter's clever sayings. Elizabeth cowers under racks of candy bars, hoping to become smaller and unseen.

Elizabeth's considerable talent as an artist should have been a boon to Sophie, who could have used it to full dramatic effect, an endless source of riches, but Elizabeth refuses to play along. Instead, Sophie mines every word of admiration from Elizabeth's art teachers for gold, stretching their simple words of praise into awestruck whisperings of reverence for the child prodigy, Elizabeth.

Elizabeth steadfastly refuses to comply with her mother's insatiable desire for significance. Elizabeth knows of her own talent: there is no question about it. She learns to draw, paint, and sculpt, and she knows her creations could be unified, whole, and lovely, but she is diligent about ruining her projects just before they are finished. Once she has witnessed its perfection, or fully imagined it in her mind, she destroys each project with some malicious movement of the brush or the knife. She simply refuses to be the raw material for her mother's gold mine.

As a high school student in central New York, Elizabeth dedicates herself to two topics: art and French. Her study of French has two substantial benefits: one is to distance herself from her mother, who is particularly averse to that language; the other is cohesion with her father and a chance to unravel his mysteries.

Even though she has a basic understanding of French from the playgrounds of Quebec, it is New York where her studies become meaningful. Her teachers introduce her to the formalities of the French language, its poetry and prose. They are thrilled with Elizabeth's growing understanding of French, and they enjoy conversing with her and creating assignments to challenge her. She never disappoints her teachers, taking on their experiments with great enthusiasm.

When Elizabeth's high school art teacher encourages her to pursue an art degree, Sophie and

Elizabeth, for once, do not disagree. Away at college, and free of her mother's constant breathing, Elizabeth studies diligently in her history and methods courses. She completes her projects and allows them to survive, even contributing various works to the student gallery at the urging of her professors.

But still her expectations differ widely from her mother's: Sophie expects her daughter to become a big star in the contemporary art world, while Elizabeth prefers to create work quietly and anonymously, using her father's name as a pseudonym. It seems Sophie's vision for her daughter will never be consonant with Elizabeth's own.

Her graduation from college, rather than a liberation or new stage of adulthood, feels like a new sort of childhood, where she must enslave herself to her economic conditions. Elizabeth cannot afford to live on her own as an artist, and she refuses her mother's offer to return home where she could live cheaply and work in her basement studio. Instead she seeks freelance assignments in graphic design for various magazines, assisting with layout, advising advertisers, and producing simple yet effective designs that please her clients immensely.

As a freelance worker, Elizabeth has a continual need to develop her client base. It is exhausting work, and she worries about losing key accounts. In this context, Elizabeth feels an acute sense that she has not fulfilled her calling as an artist. She has tired of working in counterpoint to her mother and wishes to form her own independent patterns of movement, her own rhythms, no longer in response to her mother or in defiance, but entirely her own.

> When I receive a commission, I know I should be grateful, but I detest these projects that economic necessity forces

upon me. I place another wedding photograph on the table with a sigh, and I begin to mix paints according to the colours, the brilliant reds and purples of the flowers. I fight my own will, feeling my descent into sarcasm. Instead, I must make myself into a machine – a robot programmed to produce colours and images on a canvas. It is all they have asked of me, isn't it? They didn't choose me for my creativity, but because of my compliance with the demands of past clients, my references.

I feel pressure from an ironic sense of glee: I sense possibility, deviance. It starts by expanding my pulse a bit – pushing extra blood through my veins. Perhaps my aura glows red at these moments, and perhaps this is why, after a time, I become aware of a curious silence in the apartment. I am suddenly aware, again, of the silence and solitude I live in – that accompanies me most of the time. I wonder at my mood, my veins, my tendency to repulse people without their even knowing why. But of course, I know why: because I agree to these projects, these unreal images, false notes of happiness without passion. I know what my clients think of me, what they think of artists, that like an impassive machine, I can produce, no, reproduce, some random moment, a moment selected for me, pretentious and tiresome.

I feel I should refuse to contribute to these unreasonable visions of the human condition, these contrivances, but I have been referred to this couple by other couples, and this is how I live and pay my bills. I imagine how this painting will continue into the future, hanging on some living room wall for many years into the future – reminding a family and its children of one moment of joy in its very distant past. There is a weight upon my work – the weight of an imagined community – the shame of being an outsider – unmarried yet catering to the married.

And then I think for a moment of my imaginary lover, a fantasy, so far away as to be, for me, nothing but clicks and beeps, black lines on white dots. Oh I am living a fantasy too – no more or less than these grinning two on the canvas, surrounded by flowers, looking at one another as if their own arteries would fill with nectar, as if they would drink one another for dinner. How I long to paint them with thorns rising out of the roses, scratching into their arms, with insects swarming the flowers, allergic eyes and noses.

Art supplies are expensive, and her career demands that she invest also in software and hardware as well as paints and canvases. Her friendships have dwindled since college, when she knew of like-minded artists and enjoyed discussing aesthetic theories and art history with them.

Most have gone on to marry and have children. Elizabeth feels awkward around married people, and she doesn't believe in such miracles as true love and happily ever after. She assumes that her parents' sad marriage is more typical than anyone admits.

> In my turbulent adolescence, I decided to suppress any amorous inclinations within me and avoid any sort of romance. At first it was based in cynicism and fear, later a ploy to further disappoint my mother. Now, I'm not certain of my reasons: perhaps a lack of enthusiasm and interest, perhaps an established habit of solitude. Reaching out to my imaginary lover, so far away, seems both safe and dangerous at once: safe because I can remain remote if I choose, dangerous because he is a real person with the potential of materialising before me at any moment.

The computer provides Elizabeth a sense of community that she lacks elsewhere. On her blog and her favourite travel website, she has friends. She maintains her online profiles with more care than her true-life persona. Online she chats with strangers in whom she has invested more trust than anyone she knows personally, confiding her deepest secrets.

> Deep inside me, I feel that great works of art still inhabit me, waiting for me to bring them forth. I used to attend gallery openings and museums to view great works of art and become inspired. I had friends, and I attended all of their gallery

54

openings when they lived near me, but they've all scattered around the world, and I only hope to connect with them here online. Some of us are still creating great work; others, like me, scramble for paid work that doesn't satisfy us but pays our bills. Sometimes I think my best friends are you - my distant readers - those of you who have been reading and writing with me across the distance over these years. Some of you I've met briefly, and others I never will - but you should all know that I'm grateful for your kind words and thoughts.

Elizabeth remembers feeling more lively and interesting. She remembers having a sense of relevance in the world. Now she feels disappointed when she faces her closet each morning: the same boring outfits, ever tightening on her body. She plans to lose weight, but she lacks the energy and purpose. She feels uncomfortable and self-conscious in her clothing, and she finds herself staying home more than ever. Her conversations with her parents are increasingly wearisome. Her father remains detached, and her mother pries.

When I tell my mother about my plan to travel to Morocco, there is no end to the allegorical warnings. She starts sending news articles about fraudulent marriages between Americans and would-be migrants from other countries. First this: "Elderly woman gives her children's inheritance to a handsome young swindler on her travels to Turkey." As the woman's grown

children complain of their vapourising
inheritance, the woman makes five or more
trips each year to visit her lover. This goes
on for many years until, on one of her trips,
she arrives to find her young man in bed
with another elderly woman.

Then there's this one: "American man loses
his virginity – and much more – to a
transgendered charlatan in Malaysia." A
Malaysian man poses as a gorgeous woman
to seduce an American man into marriage.
The American, exhilarated by the romance
and the promise of a subservient wife,
decides to forgive her for the phallus: it is
small, anyway, and insignificant in
relation to their love. But as soon as the
visa arrives, his spouse is gone, leaving the
American with an empty bank account and
some lingering questions.

"What do these articles have to do with
me?" I'm shouting now, waving the
clippings at my mother. "Are you calling
me a fool? What point are you making?"

I see her, doing that trick she taught me,
forcing her tongue to the roof of her mouth
and holding it there, controlling herself
from the impulse to agree, to call her
daughter a fool. Finally, she takes a deep
breath: "Elizabeth, please. I'm not accusing
you, but I have a right to be concerned. We
don't know this man. Invite him here,
where you have the safety of your own

people and familiar places. If he loves you, he will come here. He will understand your request. You shouldn't be the one to travel, especially alone." And here I almost bend because she's making a salient point. He should be the one to travel, I suppose, but there's a part of me that wants to go, apart from the idea of him. Perhaps I need a change or an adventure, something new. I'm so tired of fighting for small jobs that use my talent without helping me grow as an artist. I need to see some new places and colours, hear some new sounds – maybe learn something new about the world, about myself. See where I'm strong and where I need strengthening.

I try to remain emotionless and implacable, and my mother is reduced to stammering: "But why, darling? It doesn't make sense! Too dangerous... Impractical dream... Raped and left to die... Who can rescue you? ... Go with a friend... Take your roommate... Enjoy yourselves. You deserve a vacation. You work so hard, but why not France? Why not Italy? I can help with the expense if you want to tour galleries in Europe."

As she talks, I make mental notes for my blog – hence my fragmented memory of her words. Whether she's right or wrong, I don't think it matters. I need to find out for myself. Anyway – see how my own parents

turned out? Can I really trust their advice
on love?

Mahmoud often complains about Elizabeth to his
friends. He says that she clings to him, that she is insecure
and jealous. But with Elizabeth, he never speaks a negative
word. He is pure honey, with only words of love and
concern for her safety. He wants to know where she goes,
whom she talks to, what she does. No one has ever taken
such an interest in the details of Elizabeth's life. His
concern for her causes a large phone bill, on Elizabeth's
part, because he wants her to call him often.

Elizabeth's commitments to Mahmoud are
substantial. She has taken on extra freelance jobs to pay
for her phone bill and the packages she sends to him. She
has arranged her schedule to accommodate the time
difference between them. She sleeps at odd times – a few
hours while he teaches, a few hours later while he sleeps.
She is awake more than he is, rising early to work on
projects and staying up late to finish them. If Mahmoud
expresses a need or desire, she moves quickly to fulfil it.
She admires Mahmoud's commitment to his students, and
she feels he is underpaid and underappreciated for all his
sacrifices to the children. At first she sends packages of
books: as a poor English teacher in a small country school,
he has no way of finding and purchasing many of the
books he needs for his work. Later, emboldened by his
loving words, she sends more personal gifts – clothing,
colognes, lotions – everyday American items that seem a
luxury to him. And now, at his urging, she spends the
greater part of her savings to travel to him. She finishes
her final work assignments, parts from her precious cats,
and flies away to meet her love.

Daoud, growing up

When Daoud is a teenager, he wants very much to drive his father's car with his friends. His father often takes him out, just father and son, so Daoud can practice his driving skills, but never with other passengers and certainly not with friends. For Daoud it is not to show off the car or go on crazy adventures; instead, he is craving some tangible proof of his father's confidence. Yet his father refuses each of Daoud's requests, and if Daoud resents his father's intransigence, he keeps the feeling silently to himself.

When Daoud is finishing high school, he assumes he will study at the local university in Fez and continue to live at home with his family. But his father makes a surprising request: he wants Daoud to apply at Mohammed V University in Rabat. Daoud is elated: he has secretly longed to study at Morocco's premiere public university, with its modern, ample library and world-renowned professors. He has studied the writings from the faculty already, but the idea of attending their lectures had seemed an unattainable dream. When Daoud is accepted, his father presents him with the coveted car, on the condition that he will travel home frequently, and he arranges for Daoud to live in a small apartment near the campus.

Moved by his father's trust and generosity, Daoud excels at the university. He studies the intricacies of classical Arabic, and he becomes more fluent in English and French, not only conversationally, but as a writer. His professors are impressed with his efforts in various fields, particularly linguistics and philosophy, and he is singled out for honours on various occasions.

He makes new friends at the university: brilliant young scholars like himself who often disagree on small points in philosophy, to the delight of their professors and classmates. Together they enjoy their explorations of fine points in great depth, with references to classical Greek and Arabic philosophy as well as modern French, Algerian, and Moroccan works. These are arguments for the joy of argument – nothing contentious or personal, but simply their moment in the history of these dialogues. Everyone understands this: that even if the tone and timbre of their voices rise to an intimidating level, these young people are simply participating in a long and fascinating tradition of human thought on the human condition. Often their arguments continue at the local café after class, where they are joined by others, also offering opinions: based in history, adjusted to respond to current conditions.

As these classmates prepare to graduate, the US Peace Corps calls the chair of the Arabic department to recruit an instructor in Moroccan Arabic for the incoming volunteers. The department chair approaches his top students with the offer, and Daoud is best situated to accept. When Daoud hears he will be assigned to Kelaat M'Gouna, however, he hesitates. Rabat, where he studies, and Fez, where his family lives, are sophisticated cities, full of interesting events and companions; in contrast, Kelaat M'Gouna seems a lonely and miserable place. Sure, it might be fun to travel there for a bike tour and a look at the waterfalls. It might be nice to sit with some friends on a cliff, watching a Hollywood crew make a movie or challenge some actors to a game of pool later in the evening, but the idea of working there for any length of time, especially as the summer heat sets in, seems more a condemnation than a job.

Daoud had looked forward to a summer of festivals and concerts in Rabat, Casablanca, Fez, and Meknes. He had considered taking a few classes in Rabat with favourite professors to prepare for graduate studies. The shy young man who had left Fez at eighteen for college had become, at twenty-two, an urbane man of curious intellect, anxious to continue his studies in North African philosophy, literature, and politics, to find an angle of research in his graduate studies that will challenge the legacies of colonialism that remain obstacles to national identity and development. The idea of interrupting his studies to assist an agency of the United States runs counter to his plans and counter to his anti-colonialist stance. Isn't the Peace Corps just a vehicle for American colonialism, he wonders, and won't my participation just exacerbate the problem?

On the other hand, Daoud doesn't mind taking some time off before beginning a master's programme, and he feels he needs some real-life experiences. Perhaps he will better understand Americans and their motivations. Perhaps some time spent among the Amazigh of the south, seeing their difficulties first hand, will clarify his own positions and lend credibility to his arguments. Besides, the offer of a good salary is tempting, especially since his friends will soon be studying abroad. With such a salary, Daoud can successfully petition for a visa and travel to Europe on his vacations. With these mixed feelings, Daoud accepts the job, says goodbye to his cities, his friends, his favourite cafés, packs his father's car with books and clothing, and after a brief visit to his family, drives south towards the dusty and desolate village of Kelaat M'Gouna.

As Daoud drives on impossibly dangerous roads towards Kelaat M'Gouna, he has no idea what miracles await him there. But to meet his destiny, he must first survive the trip. On one perilous cliff-side turn, a car full of passengers nearly sends him over the edge. Daoud may feel angry, but he keeps driving. The next target is not like Daoud, and the driver does not contain his anger. When the daredevil attempts to cut in front of that car, the driver turns in towards the offending car and screeches to a halt; now the occupants of both cars fall out on all sides. Daoud, at a safe distance behind them, pulls over to wait as the fight rages: sticks, rocks, and leather whips flying in the dust. Each group tries to overthrow the other, and the cliff threatens menacingly close. After each person has given and received a beating, they all limp back to their cars. No one has died or fallen over the cliff, and each person seems equally injured.

Desert highways

The state of road repair in Morocco depends a great deal on the drivers and passengers who rely on the particular road. Because the Kelaat M'Gouna region is perpetually impoverished, the roads reflect this social condition. Larger cities are different, especially those with economic importance. When a Saudi prince builds his vacation home near Agadir, for example, he donates the money to build a pleasant highway between the airport and the city. This road has a tree-lined meridian, and stretches smoothly and evenly, without a single notch. But if you continue on this road towards Taroudant, you will know when you have reached not only the end of the benefactor's property line but also the limit of his philanthropy. The lovely meridian disappears as the bumps and potholes begin.

In 2010, a new highway from Rabat to Agadir opens with Prince Moulay Rachid cruising the distance in his cavalcade. This new highway cuts the distance between Rabat and Agadir in half by circumventing dangerous mountain passages. When we first travel this highway, it is so new that gas stations have not yet been installed. In the final fifty miles, we worry about the very real possibility that we will run out of gas before reaching the city. My beloved drives in neutral when he can coast downhill, and fortunately the path to Agadir slopes from the mountains to the sea.

It's not a terribly pressing concern, though, as car trouble in Morocco is never very troubling. When we have a problem in our car, we simply pull over; within moments we meet several kind strangers, eager to offer their help. Once, we spend a day struggling with a hot filter cap that pops off every few miles. Each time we pull over, a new set of fellow travellers stops to greet us, reaching into their trunks for canisters of water and tools. They bend their heads together to peer under our hood and solve the problem. These moments of generosity, perhaps unremarkable to Moroccans, never fail to move me.

Yet there is one night when car trouble might have troubled us. In the forests near Ifrane, our little car gives up its valiant struggle to deliver us to the royal university for a conference speech. The car had sputtered uphill all day in the heat and had finally stopped, unable to continue. Undaunted, my beloved opens the hood to check underneath, but several vehicles pass us by. "Maybe you need to come out here," he says to me, and he is right: as soon as I step out of the car, a truck loaded high with chickens pulls over. "You shouldn't stop here," they tell us, "it's very dangerous at this late hour." They wouldn't have stopped if they hadn't seen a woman, they say, as the forest is full of tricky bandits who might have staged this situation just to rob them.

As the chickens slumber soundly in the darkness, the men look over the engine together, hoping to resolve the problem quickly. After several efforts to restart the car, we only make a few metres of forward progress. Then fire erupts under the hood, and I am scrambling from the car with a laptop under each arm, visions of fiery Hollywood blasts in mind. Amid shouts, the flames blaze higher, and the men dump dirt and sand from the roadside onto the fire. My beloved has the presence of mind to ask about a fire extinguisher and is astonished when someone produces one from where it has been resting ineffectually with the chickens. Soon the fire is out, and as the chickens sleep, the men tie our car to their truck with a thick fibre rope; soon our journey to Ifrane will be realised.

Embarrassed to arrive at the royal university attached to a chicken truck, however, we worry ungraciously on our way to town. No matter: the farmers seem to understand without a word from us. They leave our car in a safe parking space and deposit us outside the royal gates. The guards are too busy with their own late-night pursuits to notice our inauspicious arrival. The next day, our colleagues warn us unequivocally: that road is full of bandits who sabotage drivers at night. Our rescuers were right to have been cautious of us, and we were lucky to have survived. We are never to use that road again – better to drive the safer route near Fez, even if it adds an hour to the trip.

Mahmoud takes things seriously

Mahmoud's classmates circle around a series of unanswerable questions about him:

"Is he ignorant or stupid?"

"Why does he want to emigrate so badly? Here he can teach and pursue his studies; there he would sweep floors!"

"Why is Mahmoud so attracted to the West?"

"How does he convince these tourists to entrust their vacations to him?"

"What do these tourists think of us, of all Moroccans, after a few days with Mahmoud?"

They debate these questions, and they lament the fact that so many tourists learn of Morocco through Mahmoud, whose verve and fervour to claw his way out of Morocco offends them. They imagine him one day squeezing into the suitcases of some unsuspecting tourists, removing their tagines and carpets to make room for himself. They imagine the shock on the tourists' faces when they open the suitcases to unpack their treasures and find instead their tour guide grinning up at them, inviting them to coffee.

Like a nomadic trader with his camels, preparing to cross the North African desert, Mahmoud wraps himself in voluminous layers that he hopes will never unravel – for Mahmoud these are layers of falsehoods, one wrapped within another. But he doesn't forget the two angels assigned to him, who write his deeds every day. These angels are both very busy, as Mahmoud does a great many deeds each day, and he tries for a balance of good to outweigh his bad.

Mahmoud has a few activities he is dedicated to: teaching high school classes, hosting tourists, and recruiting international friends on the travel site. He also pretends to be reading, writing, and preparing for graduate school in comparative literature, but if pressed, he would be unable to provide much evidence. He hopes that the internet will facilitate his marriage to a woman from Europe, Canada, or the United States so that he can migrate to her country. With his friends, he joins their laughter regarding his various women, but online he professes a deep and abiding love for a few of them, including Elizabeth. Of course, she is not the only egg in his basket, but she may be his cheapest ticket to the West, where Mahmoud imagines his scholarly career taking off. His plan isn't bad, actually. He has met enough foreign students to recognise his value as an Arabic instructor, and he hopes to build from this base a career in comparative literature. Mahmoud knows it will take diligence, intelligence, and some financial support from his parents to make his plan work, but he has just enough to make a go of it. He knows people don't approve of him, and he knows enough not to care.

When they discuss Mahmoud, people say they don't understand him. He shouldn't act like a desperate man. His family is respected in the community, and as the only son, he should be honouring his parents and preparing to manage the family business. His father owns the most prominent and best situated café in Essouaira, directly across from the central square. In fact, it has always been a place for men to get caught up on the local gossip, and it pains Mahmoud's father to become a topic for them. No one fails to notice that Mahmoud is mixing with all sorts of people from all different places, and some of his guests are unescorted young women. Mahmoud's friends are concerned: "How are these women allowed to travel alone? Don't their families care about them? It simply does not make sense."

During the week, Mahmoud lives in a small village near his school, sharing a rented room with the other male teachers. His teaching salary is small, but he doesn't mind. He gets by on the generosity of strangers, and he rarely has to ask his parents for anything. Mahmoud sleeps on a prayer mat on the floor, surrounded by these other teachers. On weekends, he travels to Agadir or Essouaira, where he visits his friends and family and enlists their help in his hosting duties.

Mahmoud maintains his image with great care. He is never seen without a book of English poetry, or a novel, or a book on literary theory. In reality, though, Mahmoud is not the lover of English he purports to be. Alone, he reads in Arabic, guiltily hiding the books in a cardboard box in his room. The first drafts of his poems are always in Arabic, then meticulously translated into English. The Arabic drafts he shreds into the tiniest of pieces.

Mahmoud's favourite volume to carry around is Homi Bhabha's *Location of Culture*, the lost property of a professor who had accepted Mahmoud's offer of hospitality for a brief time. After a few hours of being hosted by Mahmoud, the professor became so anxious to get away that he left the book behind in the taxi. Mahmoud could not have planned it better: losing the day's kickbacks was nothing compared to the value of the talisman left to him. This book has been golden for Mahmoud, who pretends that the highlighting and annotations are his own. To be seen reading such a book in the university cafeteria promotes the illusion that Mahmoud will someday reach his zenith as a university professor, perhaps in a far-off location.

Honestly, even I was momentarily impressed when I first saw Mahmoud with his dog-eared tome, highlighted in four colours, with marginalia in several languages, until I realised Mahmoud's careful construction of image above reality.

Mahmoud exploits this book to its fullest potential. If having coffee with a friend, he leaves it on the table and walks away – not far, just far enough – to order something at the counter or to talk with someone else nearby – knowing the companion will flip through a few pages to see his erudite markings. When he stands in a circle of friends, discussing some important point of philosophy, he punctuates his words by punching the air with his book. At some lull in the conversation, Mahmoud can depend on someone to ask about the book in his hand, affording him a chance to pontificate without seeming overeager.

This treasure, left for him in a taxi, gives Mahmoud an idea. He begins to write eloquent appeals to his friends overseas, pleading with them to send books by mail or to pack their suitcases with books when they travel to Morocco. Inspired by his fervent requests, his correspondents respond generously. Boxes of books arrive in the school's front office addressed to him, and his guests often bring worn books on their Moroccan vacations, knowing they will replace the books with Moroccan souvenirs for the return flight.

Who can deny a young scholar in need of books? And he flatters them by requesting books in English. Online, he describes himself in romantic desert or ocean-side settings, sipping exotic juices and reading the books he has recently received. Once he has updated his online profile to portray an earnest young scholar, he begins to attract an academic set of tourists. This Mahmoud will be the perfect host for their vacations, they feel, no need to struggle over French and Arabic translations or embarrassing errors in pronunciation. The books they send in advance of their vacations are offerings of gratitude for the guidance he will provide them.

Shall we pity these tourists? Just imagine for a moment their thoughts: to the tourist, Mahmoud is like a native English speaker, only better. The tourist was born into privilege, but Mahmoud has acquired his richness of mind on his own. He is a fan of Dickens with a sense of Moroccan hospitality – an articulate and generous guide. But tourists should consider their adjectives carefully lest they be thoroughly disappointed on their vacations. It is the tourist who adds "generous" – not Mahmoud himself. They should beware of their stereotypes and expectations regarding Moroccan hospitality. They can't expect Mahmoud to fulfil their every fantasy, and they can't obligate him to generosity no matter how they may hope for it.

Indeed Mahmoud presents himself as an excellent host to travellers, but in reality he promises more than he can deliver. The rooms he provides are often the bedrooms of displaced children or the cushions in someone's salon. When Mahmoud takes the tourist to these lodgings, he acts as if he is giving a grand tour of lavish accommodations; he speaks to the tourist as if the tourist will be very excited and grateful for the luxurious space. He leaves no room for the tourist to disagree, but it doesn't matter. He knows that he can depend on the tourist to be polite and reserve any qualms quietly within.

How they met

Who is first to notice the other, Daoud or Susan? Both claim to have been first, and each has a reasonable claim. Daoud is watching from his classroom window as the Peace Corps volunteers arrive for their first Arabic classes. His first view of Susan is obscured. She is watching the sidewalk ahead so as not to trip and fall flat. Her head is covered in a yellow scarf, but he can see her brown hair nonetheless. It isn't her face that first moves him because he can hardly see it; instead, it is the straight posture of her back even as she looks downward, and the strength and purpose he senses in her confident forward motion.

Susan's first vision of Daoud is his entrance to the classroom. He enters, loaded down with books, a spring in his step that betrays his nervousness. The sight of Daoud stops her heart and breath for a moment. He may be handsome, yes, but it isn't that: it is some sort of energy that radiates around him and makes Susan feel immediately at home.

For Daoud, the feeling is mixed: he is both happy and on edge in her presence. From this time on, Susan becomes a model student in Arabic, and Daoud wrestles with unexpected and disturbing feelings of desire.

The art of migration

Moroccan author Tahar Ben Jelloun captures the essence of Moroccan emigration when he writes of the many young people, like Mahmoud, who wish to leave Morocco for other places. Perhaps they have been disgraced at home, perhaps they have advanced degrees without employment, perhaps they wish to send money home to their families. Consider his Azel, who prostitutes himself in pursuit of the dream, who makes himself weaker and more vulnerable in his quest for a stronger position.

Ben Jelloun describes the sparkling lights of Spain that beckon from across the sea to the cafés of Tangier. For hopeful emigrants, the idea of leaving a place overwhelms every other thought. But the moment of arrival is only a moment, and a lifetime needs to follow. The emigrant can't think very far ahead. The life abroad remains illusory even as the leaving is meticulously planned.

Every Sunday at the US–Mexico border, the border patrol drives a large white bus full of deportees to the gates of the border. As the men walked off the bus onto American soil, it is clear they don't expect it to be their last time in the US. They joke with the bus driver as they collect their backpacks and cell phones, and they walk jauntily towards a white metal labyrinth that leads them back to Mexico. From a small border town, they recollect with their colleagues at a particular gas station, fill their gallons of water, and start the trek back across the fifty-mile expanse of desert. Compared to going home to southern Mexico or Central America, fifty miles north is easy, especially armed with new experiences and new information about the movements of the border patrol and the self-appointed vigilantes who guard the desert.

Moroccans don't have a desert to cross, but rather a sea. Still, they refer to the trip as a burning – in Arabic, harq: the burning of one's past to begin anew. Some years back, the border crossings between Morocco and the Spanish colonies were looser, and Moroccans could find ways to pass through the Canary Islands or the small Spanish cities inside Morocco, Ceuta and Melilla. Like the US–Mexico border crossings, security has been tightened over time, and under such conditions, migration takes a more perilous tone. In Morocco, the rumours circulate widely about the emigrants. They say that young men hang upside down from the axles of large trucks that are loading onto ferries from Tangier to Algeciras. Or that they stow away on ships, squeezing themselves into cargo boxes that will be carelessly thrown onto the ship and then off again at the Spanish port. Such stories sound like folklore to me, but I can't know for certain. In some Spanish cities, you will hear mostly Moroccan Arabic, especially in port cities such as Algeciras or Almeria. And what you may see is a vast number of Moroccans living in worse conditions than they could have imagined in Morocco. Many are victimised and destitute, without resources beyond their physical bodies.

When your feet touch Moroccan soil for the first time, you might think of all the people who are desperate to touch it for the last time, but more: think of those lost emigrants who would give anything to be home again, who will never find their way.

Mahmoud, dreamer

Mahmoud is a passionate man – everyone knows this who knows Mahmoud at all. Just yesterday, before Elizabeth's arrival, Mahmoud delivered the commencement address at the high school graduation because the graduating seniors had requested their passionate young English teacher as their commencement speaker. Mahmoud is one of those teachers who prides himself on not using lecture notes and always speaking extemporaneously. His principal, knowing this about Mahmoud, had tried rather delicately to reverse the decision of the committee, hoping for a less precarious commencement address. However, the principal had underestimated Mahmoud's popularity among the students, and when one student mentions the word censorship, the principal quickly capitulates. With a foreboding sense of dread, he asks his secretary to place Mahmoud on the programme.

As Mahmoud sits upon the stage, about to deliver his speech, he sees his parents in the front row, smiling with pride. As the principal drones on about the future of Morocco and the role of young people in their nation's development, Mahmoud drifts into a fantasy about stowing away in a wooden box to Spain. He feels the suffocating air, a choking sensation overtaking him. He imagines himself then in a tomb, buried alive, pounding on the top for someone to save him. Then he hears his name as if through a tunnel: a voice like the scratching of rats.

Mahmoud falters for a moment, disoriented. Finally he rises to the podium.

He opens with a poem, his own, celebrating the freedom of mind one can attain through literature and philosophy. Then he launches into a sentimental and patriotic speech invoking the young king, Mohammed VI, and his economic priorities, the role of young people in national development. His parents smile below as Mahmoud exhorts his students to follow in the right path and listen to the wisdom of their elders. But soon their smiles twist uncomfortably as they hear their son advocating the democratic process and rule of law. Not only his parents, but the entire crowd tenses in unison, as Mahmoud seems on the verge of calling for a democratic revolution. Then he softens his voice, murmurs some words of gratitude about the king's generous plan to create new public schools in the region, and the crowd collectively relaxes, murmuring softly together.

As soon as the ceremony ends, Mahmoud says a quick farewell to his parents, who have agreed to host his artist friend, Elizabeth, from New York. Mahmoud takes a bus to the airport in Casablanca, and his parents return home to prepare for Elizabeth's arrival.

As Mahmoud boards his bus and waves goodbye to his parents, he thinks of Elizabeth boarding her flight in New York. He has assured her that he has no interest in leaving Morocco, but of course it is not true. He wants Elizabeth to take him away from this place, where his greatest achievement is the commencement address at a small country school. He wants bigger speeches, bigger venues, his name on the cover of a book. He wants Elizabeth to rescue him from this small place and make him a larger man.

When he reaches the airport, he is vexed. There are other young men waiting expectantly for the flight from New York, and he knows what these men are about. He feels silly standing among them. Some have crude signs with a name, first name only – American names like Judy, Kathy, and Cindy. Others have outdone him; they stand looking handsome and well dressed, floral bouquets in hand. Mahmoud, having slept all night on the bus, feels awkward. He wishes he had showered and shaved.

As the women start arriving, they find their names or accept their bouquets. Mahmoud is bothered that so many women resemble Elizabeth. He approaches the wrong woman once, and then again. What troubles him more than the women resembling Elizabeth is the crowd of men resembling him, engaged in the very same dream.

First impressions

So it happens that Daoud and Susan have one of those momentous days. Do you know what I mean? One of those days that seems ordinary, but then, looking back, you realise it was a day like no other. Here we can argue our philosophies: if we have free will, it is a day of consequential ideas and decisions. If we have destiny, it is a day of God's hand moving our chess pieces around. Either way, it is a day that marks a difference: you were this person, and then you were changed.

For Daoud and Susan it is a day in June. Daoud drives a car towards his fate, as Susan boards a van in Casablanca with the other Peace Corps volunteers. For both Susan and Daoud, the first impression of Kelaat M'Gouna is the same: they enter through welcoming arches, where the Moroccan flag and the village flag wave a welcome. The town is surrounded by the Middle Atlas range of mountains, and they see snow on the highest peaks. The afternoon air feels warm. Rose-coloured homes and business structures line the entrance, all very square and vertical in keeping with the terrain of dramatic red hills and valleys. Whether the buildings look old or new, they have the same rose-coloured shade, the same squareness, the same vertical construction rising against the ridges of the natural hills. From desert to oasis, the landscape is ever-changing: on one side of the road is a lush green landscape of trees in a deep valley, a narrow stream running through; on the other side is a barren desert, a rise of red mounds, with homes seeming to grow out of them.

As Susan attends her initial orientation, Daoud becomes familiar with the language school and his classroom. They have yet to see one another, but they inhabit the same spaces now. The Peace Corps orientation includes a series of talks by the regional director and local citizens describing the many social ills affecting the region, including a powerful drug trade, prostitution, corruption, and a lack of basic services. The speakers don't mention an underground prison, and it may be true that they know nothing about it.

Brahim, a local man of twenty, is invited to speak to the new volunteers about the process of farming roses. Brahim is anxious to address the volunteers in English because he hopes that he will soon leave Kelaat M'Gouna for Kenitra where he will attend a school for tourism and hospitality.

He does his best in English to describe his family's farming operation. He explains that each family in the region has four or five plots of land dedicated to roses, and he describes each stage in the planting, irrigating, and harvesting. He tells of the three local factories that process the roses for cosmetics, oils, and spices. Brahim doesn't mention the ongoing tensions in the community, but he would like to. The farmers suspect collusion and corruption between elected officials and factory owners who keep the prices paid to farmers perpetually low. He feels that the factories should be competing for business from the farmers, and he wishes the farmers could be as organised as the factory owners seem to be. But he feels it is hopeless, and this is why he will soon be away, in Kenitra, trying to earn money to send back to his parents.

The plots of land owned by each family are rarely adjacent to one another, so the farmers spend much of their day walking among the plots of their neighbours, often carrying heavy loads of water or supplies. Brahim's family owns 76 by 40 forearms of land: he shows by his forearm how the plots are measured. He explains that the land has belonged to his family for many generations.

Brahim explains that the women are meant to stay home and care for their homes and children but that they can rarely do so: the demands of farming compel everyone to work side-by-side in the ploughing, irrigating, planting, harvesting, and extracting of seeds for the next cycle. Besides the roses, the families plant food for themselves and their animals. Many of the men take second jobs as masons and factory workers.

Brahim is proud that his region is the only one in Morocco where roses are farmed and processed. He voices a few concerns without assigning blame: "We are paid only one dirham for a kilogram of roses," he says, "a lot of strangers come and steal our roses without realising how much it hurts us."

Once Susan begins the fieldwork, she realises the agonising pain that the farmers endure, and she sees how the men and women work in equal measure. Even if women are said to be in charge of the harvest, the men work alongside them; even if men are in charge of irrigation, everyone is carrying buckets. Life on these farms is in continual motion, from the rise of the sun until long after it sets. And yet for all their work, there is very little reward. Without hospitals and clinics, many women die in childbirth, and a simple illness can carry a death sentence. The closest school is kilometres away, and the children must cross a river with no bridge to go there.

There isn't a dentist in the region, so they suffer needlessly and constantly as their teeth rot steadily away. Susan becomes obsessive about her own teeth. She writes to her parents for extra toothbrushes, floss, and fluoride rinse. Guiltily, she hoards these items, sneaking away several times each day to brush, floss, and rinse. She knows by sharing these items she might save people from some pain, but she is fearful of sharing lest her supplies dissipate too quickly. Though this hoarding is a point of shame for Susan, she finds she cannot stop herself.

Susan is determined to work alongside the farmers in the fields, to learn the details of their work. She learns to plan, to provide just enough water without waste, to harvest and bundle the kilos for the factory. It surprises her how far apart the family plots are, and she wonders why the families don't trade plots to save time.

She can't understand why the farmers don't bargain collectively to demand better prices from the factories. Susan's father belongs to a very successful trade union, and she remembers well when they voted to strike. Susan was fourteen, and the uncertainty of the strike felt unsettling for Susan and her sister, but within two weeks, the workers celebrated a victory, and her family's economic situation improved.

Susan harbours many ideas about how things could be better for the villagers, but when she mentions her thoughts to the field director, she is cautioned to respect the local customs and not interfere. The Peace Corps has made several disastrous miscalculations lately, and it is in a mode of self-preservation since various projects around the world have gone awry: invasive trees improperly planted in the Dominican Republic, wells in Cambodia that may have accidentally tapped into arsenic, CIA operatives discovered among the volunteers. For these reasons, the Peace Corps is in a conservative mood, and Susan's activism is not welcome.

Susan had volunteered for the Peace Corps because of a personal sense of optimism and a desire to make a meaningful impact on an unjust world, and yet here, faced with a real set of problems, she is told not to meddle. The social and economic problems that Susan witnesses in Kelaat M'Gouna vex her quite incessantly, and she occasionally disobeys her director to mention her ideas to the women, who gently laugh and brush her words aside.

The idea of collective bargaining is not as innovative as Susan thinks. The farmers have tried to organise formally in the past, but they have all experienced deep betrayals: the factories have paid certain farmers to act as spies and conquer any collective efforts. And this is why the women insist on keeping their traditional plots, why they continue to inconvenience themselves, walking long distances with buckets of water: as they walk back and forth between the plots, they see one another, and they talk. Most of their talk is friendly, but they also pass messages back and forth, and there is a great deal of honest discussion, exposing evidence of corruption between factories and politicians. Even if each farmer must go alone to the factory to sell roses, the farmers have found a collective solution that holds them gently together. It is not the villagers, but rather Susan, who must adjust to new ideas.

Enigmae

One February in Morocco, it rains for many days: a steady, unrelenting downpour. In the history of keeping track, such rain has never been recorded in Morocco. We cancel our appointments from Tangier to Taroudant, as the roads become feral rivers, rushing to sea, carrying all they can tear away and all they can hold. Bridges go to sea, and walls and windows, tables, cushions, even refrigerators and cars. The Atlantic Ocean grows to a tall, muddy, churning mountain. We watch it, concerned it could rush back towards us or assail us with its wreckage, but it never does, choosing instead to settle within itself. When the rains stop, there are roads to repair and homes to rebuild. Within months, seeds that had lain dormant under desert sands for decades sprout, and the deserts bloom in green, purple, yellow, and white. The parks become so lush and thick that the pathways disappear, and delicate flowers stand in our way, sentries against our treading feet.

Like the rains of that February, my beloved and I are enigmatic to one another. His words often surprise me, as mine do him. He thinks he would like me to be more predictable, but I don't believe it, as he is so easily bored.

During that glorious, rain-soaked month, we stay alone together inside a warm hotel room, looking outside the window at the pouring rain, the debris passing along the road, the swollen ocean bay, and my poem to him is a page covered in "yes". Sometimes we need to look deep within each other, undistracted by anything else, to remember our first and most abiding commitments. I feel, sometimes more strongly than others, a compelling and potent sense of "yes". I know him sometimes in an old way, and then I learn about him in a new way, and "yes" feels good, and true.

Mahmoud, misunderstood

Mahmoud would have preferred to take Elizabeth to another place, not his family's home. He needs some time alone with Elizabeth, to convince her of his love. At home, he knows that his parents will expect too much of his relationship with Elizabeth. His mother will be overly solicitous, and his father overly gracious. He expects his sisters to be unkind – friendly and accommodating on the surface, but insulting behind her back. She isn't beautiful in the way that they are, and they won't want to walk around the village with her. She'll spend too much time at home alone.

Of course, Mahmoud can't walk around the neighbourhood with her without causing a great deal of unnecessary gossip, and his father won't allow it anyway. As owner of the local café, Mahmoud's father provides space for the gossip of others, and he often cautions his family that he doesn't want to be a topic in these conversations. For this reason, Mahmoud is watched carefully by his two sisters, and their strict vigilance regarding his whereabouts and activities is not only tolerated by his parents but encouraged. Many times has Mahmoud been called out or punished for creating scandals, even when news from another city improbably reaches the ears of his family. Mahmoud often feels indignant. He's a young man with a bit of a wild streak, and he likes to have fun and be sociable. He can't always predict the results, and he resents the way news travels ahead of him.

For example, how could he have known that those women he befriended on the university campus were prostitutes? They had been hanging around with the Saudi students, and Mahmoud had simply answered their questions about good restaurants in the area. Is he to be blamed because they invited him along? And if he had a small drink of wine just as one of his cousins happened to pass by the restaurant window, so what? Is the world coming to an end because he had a drink of wine? How could he refuse their hospitality? Once his sisters get wind of this episode, however, they can't let it go. Several weeks pass, and still they discuss it, reminding him that Ramadan will soon come and catch him unclean and unprepared. Even after he apologises for embarrassing his parents, they continue to remind him of his failures and impending doom.

Last year, Mahmoud had access to a large home in Marrakesh from a man who had wanted to marry Mahmoud's sister, Naima. Blinded by love, as so often happens, the man makes a foolish decision, entrusting the keys of his house with Mahmoud before departing Morocco for two years to study for a master's degree in England.

Silly Mahmoud. Had he been a moderate man, he could have used this house for two years. But moderation is not Mahmoud's specialty.

It isn't easy for the man's neighbours to track him down in London, but the crowds of foreigners, coming and going at all hours, distress them. They call the police, who offer no assistance, and then they find the man's number in London. The man has to send several cousins to the house to rout Mahmoud and the twenty-five foreign tourists inside: some that Mahmoud had invited online, some extras that he had picked up at the airport, and even a few that he had pulled in from the market where they had been haggling unsuccessfully for carpets and lamps.

The man doesn't want his cousins to have the keys to his house either, but he had been foolish to trust Mahmoud. From then on, he worries each night about the state of his home and his properties, finding it difficult to concentrate on his studies. Of course, Mahmoud's sister is furious about losing her best marriage prospect, and though Mahmoud continues to defame the man and deny the accusations, Naima will never forgive her brother.

It is becoming more difficult for Mahmoud to host foreign tourists: as the tourist's plane is touching land, he is still scrambling to find a place for the tourist to stay. He calls upon friends, acquaintances, distant family members, and even friends of his parents. Increasingly he has been meeting his guests at the airport in Agadir with excuses: a younger brother has fallen ill or a distant relative has surprised him with a visit. Now Mahmoud suggests a hotel where he knows the manager. The manager will give the tourist an excellent deal. Later, Mahmoud will come to the hotel to take the tourist around: they will visit the market, see the ocean from the hilltop and the boardwalk, ride a camel. In each of these locations, money changes hands. Mahmoud receives commissions from every person who receives money from the tourist: the hotel manager, the merchants at the market, the owners of camels and cafés.

When Elizabeth arrives, Mahmoud has exhausted many of his resources. No one is willing to host Mahmoud's new American guest. Somewhat apprehensively, he asks his parents to host her: an American artist, he says. He knows the risks: his mother will be suspicious of a single woman travelling alone, and the neighbours will say unkind words behind her back.

heArtblog, Sept 15

We have travelled by bus to Mahmoud's family – long hours on the bus, but these hours have been good for us, and necessary. I have learned more about Mahmoud in these hours than I had been able to learn in the many months of our disembodied conversations. There are some things that cannot be conveyed electronically.

Sitting next to a person, getting used to his smell, the feel of his hands, the third dimensions of him – how his face looks when he hasn't shaved it, the low and halting sound of his voice, as he hesitates over English pronunciations. Perhaps it is wrong of me that I still haven't spoken to him in French, as I know it would be easier for him, but I feel that I must keep some things to myself for now. Even this blog is still a secret from him, but he will learn of it someday, when I'm ready.

Here we are now at his family home, together, and I can confirm all my feelings about him. And yes, as I suspected, I love him. I love his smell – some sort of musky sweetness. I love his touch, so gentle and careful. His sweet voice – not as confident as I had imagined. In fact, he seems more fragile and vulnerable than I had expected – as if there are tears just behind his words, tears that he might let fall someday. After so many months, we are finally united, and though surrounded by other people, we exist within our own small space, entirely alone.

Public and private tragedies

In a 15th century civil war, the sultan gives his children to the Spanish monarch in exchange for military assistance against his enemy – his brother. When the sultan emerges victorious, he owes a great debt to his Spanish allies. He wants his children back; the Spanish want Larache, a strategic fortress on Morocco's northern Atlantic coast. The sultan, anxious to justify what he expects to be an unpopular transaction, writes to the scholars in Fez, requesting a religious fatwa that grants him permission. Some scholars leave the mosque in protest and flee to the south, while others comply with the royal request. Larache is gifted to the Spanish, and the royal parents are reunited with their children.

Approximately five hundred years later, the sultan's descendant, King Hassan II, has an elaborate birthday party, a party that is interrupted by a violent *coup d'état* led by palace insiders. Even though the interior minister, an orchestrator of the coup, is killed on the scene, the crime must be fully avenged to dissuade any others who might be considering a similar attempt against the king. He imprisons the man's wife and young children, sending them from their residences within the royal palace to one of the most cruel and austere prisons of the desert, Tazmamart, where they starve and suffer for twenty years.

When Susan first hears of these prisoners she is seated in a café with other Peace Corps volunteers. Susan is just beginning to make sense of Moroccan Arabic, so she overhears this hushed conversation incompletely. The men in the café speak of children in prison, children of important leaders, starving and sickly children who had once lived wealthy and pampered in the royal palace. Susan, disbelieving, imagines these men are inventing a story or retelling the storyteller's tale from last night's gathering on the square. She does not imagine the men are discussing real people or real events. Besides, the café is crowded, and her friends chat noisily in English. She is eager to ask her Arabic instructor, to see what he knows about this story.

When she finds Daoud, just before class, her question makes him visibly upset. He takes her by the elbow, and they move away, still within sight of the others milling around the lobby of the language institute but out of their range of hearing. Maybe Daoud's response alarms Susan, but it excites her too. She has an amiable relationship with her Arabic instructor, but he keeps a respectful distance. In truth, she harbours a secret and potent crush on Daoud that often keeps her awake at night and follows her into her dreams. She hopes he hasn't noticed how nervous she becomes in his presence.

Daoud has noticed. He too struggles to keep his composure with Susan, and he regrets his cold demeanour to her; it is a coldness he doesn't feel, but he maintains it nevertheless. Not for a moment would he consider a romantic relationship with a woman from outside his country, nor would he marry a non-Muslim, and certainly not an American. Daoud knows he will marry someone from a family his parents have always known well, and this marriage is far into the future, after his studies, after his professional career has been securely set in motion. Every day he fights against the feelings he has for Susan. He considers this a contest of will, perhaps a test from God.

Mahmoud and his sisters

Sisters can be complicated. Even though Mahmoud can predict his sisters fairly accurately, as he has done by necessity throughout his life, he can't always win; in fact, he hardly ever does.

"Mahmoud, we need to talk to you," says one. It doesn't matter which, because they speak with a unified voice and purpose.

"Busy," he mutters, trying to avoid their conflict. He is dressed and ready for market, and he has almost escaped the house, but his two sisters confront him and block his way.

"Not so fast, little brother. Take this woman with you if you are going."

"She's tired. She had a very long flight. Let her stay here and read or draw pictures or whatever she wants to do. Take care of her. I promised Mama I would get some things from the market."

"Quit lying, Mahmoud. Mama sent Nourma for bread and eggs already, and she doesn't need anything else. Sit down here for a minute." Mahmoud knows when his two older sisters mean to subdue him. He still has marks from their sharp fingernails on his face and arms. He sits awkwardly on the edge of a cushion. "Mahmoud," begins Naima, "This girl is a disgrace. She has no beauty, no figure, and no brains. If she had two grams of brain in her head, Mahmoud, she would not have come here to meet you."

"Look at you!" Fatiha interrupts her sister, "You have nothing to offer her! You sleep on a dirty floor all week with a group of poor men like you."

Now Naima again, "You, Mahmoud, who has so much promise. You are nothing but a village schoolteacher. It is time for you to start a real career."

And now her sister, "Then you can think of marriage, but marry someone our parents know— your second cousin is a good match for you."

"But he doesn't want her! She is too sweet and nice for his taste. He can't get his mind off that Zahra."

"Zahra! The one he tried to feel up on the bus when they were little kids? He was ten years old and so fresh! She slapped him, remember? So hard he had a mark on his face! Zahra would never have him."

"That's a lie!" Now they have stepped over a line, and Mahmoud has to defend himself. "It's a lie – I just bumped her!"

"Don't interrupt, Mahmoud. Zahra will never have you."

Mahmoud makes a quick move to the door, but his sisters are faster. He no longer keeps track of which sister says what:

"Mahmoud, look at yourself!"

"We are serious with you."

"Our mother is facing taunts and gossip through the neighbourhood because of you and this stranger."

"She will be a constant burden to you as long as she stays here."

"And she has nothing for you in New York; nothing to offer you."

"We saw all the chats on your ridiculous website, Mahmoud."

"What a disgrace!"

"Pathetic."

"You, who has so much talent!"

"What a shame!"

When Mahmoud finally manages to escape the verbal clutches of these sisters and runs towards the market to meet his friends, he recalls their fierce childhood fights, when their words were fewer but sharper, and their insults assaulted him from two sides. He was never a match for these sisters, who had various strategies to beat him. If they could not win by humiliating him, they could easily overpower him physically. If that didn't work, they could tattle and lie about him, always two against one, and as a boy he was held responsible, no matter his innocence in the matter.

Now, however, he can see his advantage. How can they bully him regarding Elizabeth? What can they say to his parents that his parents don't already know? Is there any bit of gossip about Mahmoud that isn't already circulating with merciless enthusiasm through the neighbourhood? What new gossip can his sisters contribute to the conversation: That Elizabeth is unattractive? That he is using her in a dishonourable way? It has all been said before.

Mahmoud may feel ashamed of himself and his relationship with Elizabeth, but not more so because of his sisters. He shakes himself a bit, as if to shake off the dreadful feelings, and then he continues on to the café where he will meet Najib and Abdelmajid, where they will drink coffee before heading to the market.

He knows they too will laugh and try to shame him, but Mahmoud knows he can laugh at them too. They have no hope of leaving this town, and Mahmoud, for the first time, can see a door opening before him. He will push until it opens, and soon he will step through and away. And this is no Moroccan door of ornate carved wood or inlaid tile but rather an American door made of steel and plastic, a door that will seal him inside the pressurised cabin of a Boeing 747.

New York is only a short way from Harvard University, where the great Homi Bhabha imparts his wisdom to his privileged assemblies. Mahmoud imagines himself in the scholar's majestic office, receiving his benefactor's praise and advice. In this fantasy, Dr Bhabha insists that Mahmoud continue writing poems; he offers to supervise Mahmoud's doctoral thesis. Then, this business settled, Dr Bhabha eases back into his large and comfortable chair, asking to hear another, another, and yet another of Mahmoud's poems. Dr Bhabha, overwhelmed and inspired by Mahmoud, proclaims him successor to the long history of great poets writing in Arabic. "I'll make a few calls for you," says the Dr Bhabha of Mahmoud's dreams. "You will need a good agent, the best. I know one in New York who has connections through the Arab world, and in Paris, of course."

Mahmoud has finally embarked on his journey to magnificence, and all of this is due to Elizabeth. He feels a warm sense of gratitude towards her, and for a moment he hopes his mother will be kind to her. His mother knows his ambition, and he hopes she will forgive him for following this unsavoury path to success.

Susan sees beauty and other concerns

June, 1990

When I first meet Nora, she is walking along on the dusty road leading to the city gates of Kelaat M'Gouna. Sometimes I wonder when these gates were constructed – it could have been last year or a thousand years ago. Sometimes there are masons who come to repair holes in the red clay walls.

But Nora doesn't seem to notice the gates as she keeps her eyes low. When I greet her, though, "Asalam 'alaykum," I think my strange accent must amuse her. She looks up with a shy and lovely smile, and she greets me, too: "'Alaykum salam."

Nora is a child, but her responsibilities in her family are great. Like a grown woman, Nora wears the typical black headscarf fastened tightly with a knot at the back of her head and another, larger, black scarf tied at one shoulder, enveloping her entire body from shoulder to knees. Like a child though, she wears a Hello Kitty T-shirt under the draping scarf, with sweatpants in spite of the heat. Her only nod to the summer are the flip-flops on her feet.

Nora's ready smile belies a terrible grief.

Just three months ago, her father, a strong and resourceful farmer, discovered a small growth on his tongue. This sore festered and grew for two months, until suddenly the man was dead. The end of her father's life has meant the end of Nora's childhood. Nora, who had always held the top place in her class, has quit school to work alongside her mother in the market. Nora's teacher is devastated, too. Her best pupil could have earned a scholarship to the university in Agadir. Fluent in Tamazight, Moroccan Arabic, Classical Arabic, French, and English, whose recitation of the Qur'an is particularly impressive, Nora could have excelled in various fields.

The neighbours are concerned about the family because the young widow has five children; the unexpected death has left the family in ruins.

What makes me angry, furious, is that this simple illness could have had a simple cure. It was a small sore in a man's mouth! Back home, a dentist would have known what to do, would have made it go away.

The lack of medical clinics in the region has created a population of widows and orphans, and why? No one can answer for this.

Nora had been her father's close companion. As his oldest child, she often accompanied him to the queen coronation at the Festival of Roses. This year, her father had expected Nora to be crowned, but now Nora tells me that the festival is boring: same musicians, same dancers, same arguments, year after year. I wonder what she means when she says that the festival is boring: is she a typical bored teenager? Or is this a symptom of depression? No matter, I suppose. Until medical and dental concerns are addressed, what hope is there for mental health care?

The festival is all anyone talks about these days. Honestly, I'm not sure what to expect. On one hand, it sounds like a home-grown, grassroots, community festival; on the other hand, the community depends on multinational corporations as sponsors – Coca-Cola, Renault, and television channels from Rabat, Dubai, and Paris. Is the festival an economic boon for the community, as people think? Or are the profits moving elsewhere? If this festival brings money to the region, then where is it? Wouldn't it go first to health and education, the primary concerns of the people? The children walk several kilometres to school, and there is no bridge over the river. They must walk through the water, fighting its currents, on their way to school and home again. When the river is high, only a few of the older children attempt to cross. Couldn't the money from the festival be used for some basic needs of the community – a bridge over the river, perhaps? How hard could it be?

And another thing – this beauty contest – why do they do it? It seems contrary to their values. Why would these women, who dress in black scarves, covering themselves from head to toe, approve of a beauty contest? It just doesn't make any sense, and they call it by an English name: "Queen of Roses." When I hear the teenagers talk, it is all about the coronation, and always in French, as if they don't want their parents to understand. And just like in the States, there are two basic responses to a beauty contest: bored indifference and clandestine campaigning. How familiar this is to me! I would have been the girl feigning bored indifference, while my sister would have been a chattering gossip, betraying her ambitions to the crown.

I'd like to look forward to the festival, I really would. I hear of exciting concerts and carnival rides, but then I hear of fights that often swell in the heat of the festival afternoons. The festival brings tourists, some who consider the Rose Festival their annual foray into the forbidden. There is whispered gossip about prostitution, drug abuse, and violence.

I told Professor Daoud how I was feeling about the festival, and he said he was feeling the same – unsettled. He wants to go home to Fez and avoid the whole thing. Then he offered to take me to Fez, too. He said that his sister and his parents would enjoy meeting me and would host me at their home. I'm nervous, excited, thrilled. Should I go? Of course, of course not, of course. What a strange expression. Yes, I'm going.

Daoud is quietly thrilled when Susan confesses her discomfort with the festival. He's been feeling the same way. He's been a little homesick, too, wanting to see his friends and family. Here's the reality: Daoud is often invited to Fez, Rabat, Agadir, and other places on the weekends. His friends miss him, and they don't understand his immobility. Daoud can't leave Kelaat M'Gouna, and he can't tell anyone why. He can't leave because of Susan: he can't invite her, and he can't go without her. When Susan mentions her misgivings about the festival, Daoud recognises an opportunity and a perilous moment. He takes a deep breath and delivers the words he has been rehearsing for days: "Would you like to see Fez and meet my family?" And Susan, who would like nothing more than this, falters a bit as she stammers out her yes. "I would like that very much, thank you." In the history of Daoud and Susan, from their easy conversations in the language school to their fluid marital dialogues much later, whether gentle or contentious, this invitation and response is the only conversation they ever struggle to deliver.

Daoud and Susan decide to stay in Kelaat M'Gouna just long enough to see the transformation of the town into its carnival atmosphere and the arrival of the first tourists. As they drive away in Daoud's father's car towards Fez, they see young men lined up along the roadside, holding long strings of roses they will sell as necklaces. Daoud pulls over, runs across the street against the incoming traffic, and buys three necklaces. One he gives to Susan immediately, and the other two he saves for his sister Amal and his mother.

As they drive along narrow mountain roads, against traffic, the car somehow clinging to the sides of each cliff, the fragrant smell of roses infusing the air, Susan thinks of Nora and her mother at the market. She hopes for the smallest of wishes, that Nora and her mother earn enough to feed their family of six for a few extra weeks. The modesty and humility of this simple wish aligns with the severity of the landscape in which Susan has found herself. Just a short time ago, she wished for luxuries – vacations and new clothing. But now her expectations for the world and its offerings have scaled back dramatically. She no longer thinks in general terms about world peace: instead she hopes for specifics: healthy teeth and an equitable distribution of food. When President Kennedy proposed the Peace Corps, he had expected young people to be changed by the experience, and for Susan, it has introduced her to the stark realities of poverty in a way that her studies could not have done.

As the dusty highway begins to level out, closer now to Fez, Amal and her parents prepare for Daoud's visit, puzzled by his cryptic phone call. He has told his father that he will bring a guest: a woman, a foreign woman. Not only is his family curious: the whole neighbourhood awaits the arrival of Daoud and his unusual guest.

Daoud is close with his family and neighbours. Even in Rabat, where pretty and intelligent women are always in close proximity, Daoud maintains a polite and respectful distance. He simply doesn't want to be distracted from his studies. He expects his eventual marriage will be something engineered by his parents, something he will acquiesce to rather than seek for himself.

When Susan's presence begins to distract Daoud, he is perturbed, and not necessarily pleased. When he invites her to Fez, he would like very much to believe that he acts rashly and imprudently, but he knows better than to be dishonest with himself. The truth is that he is, in spite of his best intentions, falling in love with Susan, and this fact is a problematic if inspiring reality. He invites Susan home not on a whim, but because he cannot imagine going home without her. He hopes that his parents can help him to make sense of his new situation.

Rose festival
anthropology

Fifteen years after Daoud and Susan escape from the Rose
Festival, my beloved and I go willingly towards it. The
Rose Festival, held in Kelaat M'Gouna each May to
celebrate the harvest of roses, began officially in 1962; the
local people, however, claim the festival is much older, a
tradition of their ancestors that has always been.

When we first hear of the Rose Festival of Kelaat
M'Gouna, we hear that it is a nice local gathering with
music, theatre, foot races, parade, queen coronation, and
carnival. Local products are sold there: cosmetics, oils,
lotions, and spices derived from roses. It seems
prototypical as a festival, a useful object study for two
anthropologists.

As we drive towards the village, we see the streets
lined with children – dozens of young people standing still
on the side of the road with their arms outstretched,
holding thick necklaces made of roses in varying lengths.
These are full and fragrant bunches of roses they have
created themselves from their family plots – soft and
lovely, a warm welcome to the festival.

We arrive early on the first day, a Friday. Two
months earlier, historic rainfalls had swept this land, and
fresh, small tufts of green poke out from the dry desert
sands. The sun is only beginning to rise from the horizon,
but the streets are crowded with an international array of

pedestrians. We watch as a police officer collects a bribe from a driver and waves him past the roadblock.

The town is decorated in rosy pink: with roses and rose-coloured products, a Ferris wheel spinning on a distant hill. Musicians arrive, instrument cases in hand.

The festival is still hours from starting, yet every chair in every restaurant is occupied. Locals are in no hurry to leave their seats, as they sip coffee, talk with their friends, and laugh, watching the crowd thicken in the streets. There are others like us, some with cameras, others with notebooks, making a record of this day. Tourists wander slowly, a bit uncertain about how to engage with the festival. Because there are various organising bodies, it is difficult to know where everything is happening and when. For example, a young man approaches us with a flyer, inviting us to a play that he and his friends are producing. We would like to find a programme that would advertise all the events of the festival, but there is no such thing.

My idea is to record storytellers and musicians, although my beloved believes there is more to these festivals than what we see on the surface. As we begin our interviews with local villagers, we soon learn that he is right. In fact, our participants do not want to talk about folklore or traditions. Instead, they want to tell us about corruption in the processing plants, how the price for their roses is fixed, and their unmet demands for education and health care. Folklore is distant to them, but their daily stories are real and immediate: corrupt city officials in collusion with factory owners to underpay the rose farmers. Powerful madams who control the sexual tourism of the region and force young women to submit to prostitution. People dying from diseases that should have simple cures. Children who must cross a river with no bridge each day if they want to go to school.

When they do talk about the festival and its traditions, we realise that they are doing it to please us, and when we really listen, we hear that they are talking in metaphors. Music, for example, becomes a metaphor for the cultural divide between Arab and Amazigh peoples. The local musicians perform as the ancestors did, in Tamazight, while the outsiders come to sing to them in Arabic. They feel that the Arabic music is meant to pacify them, while the Tamazight songs are a call to consciousness. If a conflict begins, it starts with the music, dissonant clashes between chords, and this inconsonance is mirrored in the Amazigh–Arab conflicts that often erupt at the festival. Sometimes the clashes are so violent that city officials vow to close the festival forever. The only way that the festival survives each year is that the village women rally to save it.

The festival has always been considered an economic boon to the community, but the people are becoming less sure about its benefits. They complain that international companies have begun to sponsor the festival, and so the profits that the festival once provided to the community have been diverted away. They say that there are too many visitors now from the USA, Europe, and the Gulf, too many who are taking without giving.

Hassan, like most of the local people, is Amazigh. He is thirty-one years old, dressed in a typical outfit for men of the region: western trousers, button-down shirt unbuttoned over a T-shirt, plastic sandals. Also typical for this region, his hands and feet are deeply calloused and his teeth badly decayed.

When we ask him about the music at the festival, he says, "What brings fame to the festival is the prostitution, not the music."

Hassan says the festival supports about one hundred prostitutes, and that twenty prostitutes work in the village year-round. He believes prostitution is the only lucrative business left in the region, the most powerful draw for the tourists we see around us. He says the women come from the surrounding villages in the Middle Atlas, sometimes because their families send them to work in the rose fields, sometimes to escape a difficult marriage. He says they come to town on the bus, and madams are at the station to meet them. He points out two women strolling towards us. "Prostitutes," he says. We see them: in contrast to most women of the region who are lean and small, these women are full-figured, walking with a big show of confidence – unveiled, with big framed sunglasses, their long hair swinging jauntily behind them. Rather than the loose skirts and jellabiyas of the farming women, they wear tight black pants with colourful, flowing blouses.

Hassan plans to marry soon. He knows of a woman in a distant village whom he hopes will have him. He has travelled far to find a wife because he wants her to be completely dissociated from the region. He fears that a local woman would escape to her family when angry or towards prostitution when bored. He wants a hard-working woman who will help his mother in the fields. Soon he will travel with his father to Taroudant to make his formal proposal. He hopes that his mother will like her.

Mohamed, who owns the small hotel where we stay, makes his living from tourism and yet has a keen sense of the drawbacks. "Kelaat M'Gouna has many hotels," he says, and he points to the irony. "No hospital, no school, but so many hotels, all filled with prostitutes, drugs, and alcohol. We have plenty of drugs here, but nothing to cure us." When he says, "We are being colonised again, this time by tourists," I remember reading Jamaica Kincaid's treatise on tourism, *A Small Place*. I realise we have landed in a place like she describes, where tourists enjoy their impunity, acting in ways they never would at home.

Sometimes we drive along the winding roads around Kelaat M'Gouna, and we see a film crew from Germany or maybe Hollywood. Movies are often filmed in Morocco, even if they are set in other places. Ouarzazate, with its film studios, provides a base from which camera crews venture out towards any one of Morocco's forests, beaches, or deserts. A diversity of climates and landscapes provides for every type of setting that a film director may require.

Sometimes, as we drive the narrow roads, we meet tourists on bicycles. The natural beauty of the area includes waterfalls through the gorges, the red desert spotted by green oases, cliffs towering above lively streams.

Once, as we travel through the Dades Gorges, the bus in front of us stops abruptly. The line of traffic has been moving slowly, but now we have reached an impasse. Between a wall of rock and a wide stream, a tourist bus faces an equally wide truck, and there is no room for them to pass one another. The truck is piled fifteen feet high with hay, on top of which is a platform holding a flock of sheep: we can see the curly locks of the herd tottering well above our heads, with a shepherd there, too, keeping watch. From his vantage point, he probably saw this deadlock coming, but he would have been incapable of communicating the impending disaster to his driver. The bus they face is filled with Israeli tourists.

Had they been the only two vehicles on the road, it could have been a simple conflict between two drivers, and the more relaxed of the two would have moved in reverse to allow the other an easy passage. But it is certainly not simple. There are dozens of cars and trucks following each of the vehicles. One entire line of vehicles needs to back up enough to allow either the bus or the truck to pass through. It will be the sheep with their Arab driver and shepherd or the Israeli tourists. The Amazigh crowd will need to decide which side to support because it will be the Amazigh on foot who will direct the line of traffic to back up.

It is hard to tell who is most uncomfortable here: the sheep and shepherd towering above, the tourists on the bus, or the farmers on the ground. The bus is surrounded, everyone shouting suggestions to the drivers in various unfamiliar languages. Even well intentioned and benevolent shouting can sound threatening to the foreign ear.

The situation seems impenetrable: no one knows what to do. Not one of the tourists descends from the immobile bus, even though they are invited to step out and wander around. There are walking paths near the water, farmers selling vegetables and handmade crafts, a pleasant restaurant where everyone could relax and listen to the waterfall. Yet the moment is peculiar and unsettling. On the one hand, we wish the tourists would stretch their legs, walk around a bit, resign themselves to the fact that their bus won't move forward for hours. On the other hand, we are relieved when they stay safely inside. Are they imprisoned here, in a self-contained capsule, or do they choose to remain locked away together?

On this day, while the traffic stands still, Amazigh flags fly everywhere, some high on poles, others draped around people as capes. The flag has three bright, wide stripes of turquoise, green, and yellow with a red figure in the centre representing the human spirit. The students of a local school and its teachers are on a class outing to the gorges, and they are using this day, some time away from the school building and its strictures, to celebrate Amazigh heritage. They line up facing one another to dance, play drums, and sing.

Noureddine is one of the students, but he is much older than the others. Although he is twenty-one years old, he is still in high school, three years behind his intended graduation date. Since the death of his father, six years ago, Noureddine has struggled to finish high school. Often when the river is high, he cannot cross with his sister to attend. Recently, however, he has acquired a bicycle, so that he and his sister can ride together. He stands, pushing the pedals, while she sits behind him, holding tightly to his waist. The river has been low for some time, and so finally this year he will graduate. He proudly maintains his place as salutatorian, second in his class.

Noureddine has become an activist for Amazigh rights. He has begun to create dreadlocks in his hair, and he drapes an Amazigh flag over his orange T-shirt and jeans. When he speaks, he twists his hair. He wants to tell us about his life and the struggles of his family. As an activist, he has expanded his sociological imagination enough to understand that his own life story can serve as an allegory for others, for foreigners and outsiders, to understand the plight of his people.

Noureddine is small and thin; he lives alone with his mother and youngest sister, where they farm plots of roses and vegetables.

He tells us how a simple illness, or a complicated childbirth, usually carries a death sentence in Kelaat M'Gouna. He says the region does not have the necessary conditions to support a healthy lifestyle. He tells of the death of his father, who was not desperately ill but died nevertheless. It began with a small growth inside his mouth that was neither diagnosed nor treated; like Nora's father many years ago, the sore in his mouth grew for several months, becoming more and more painful, until it killed him. Given an adequate health care system,

Noureddine is convinced that his father, and others with similar untreated illnesses, could have easily recovered.

Besides the lack of health care, Noureddine is angry about other conditions. He and his mother work long days in the fields, yet they can hardly pay their utility bills. Like Hassan and others have said, Noureddine believes that elected officials and factory owners fix the prices on the roses, deflating the price each year.

Noureddine claims that the conditions of the region don't improve because the people don't examine the issues deeply or demand their rights. He says that women are idealistic, pressuring the men to become wealthy, but the region has neither wealth nor conditions for building it.

Political activism means forfeiting safety for the common good, and he is willing. He has been to jail and suffered beatings by police. He says, "I'll go to jail to defend human rights, that's fine with me, as long as I do nothing that I know to be wrong in my heart."

In the previous year, he joined street protests with students from the university in Agadir. They closed down the main street of Kelaat M'Gouna, blocking traffic, waving Amazigh flags, and making speeches. After Noureddine joined the protests, his older brother did, too. Their mother supported them by bringing food, as did many of the women of the community.

When officials and auxiliary forces arrived to disperse them, the protesters requested a frank and honest discussion about the responsibilities of government, but this discussion was not to be. Instead, the police arrested the students from Agadir, taking them to custody in Ouarzazate. They sent the locals home, but only after giving each of the protesters a solid beating to warn them from further activism. The police may have ended the protests in the street, but not in the mind of Noureddine. For him, the protests continue, and they will, until his community has clinics with dentists and doctors, city officials are called to task for corruption, and children have schools on both sides of the river.

Mahmoud goes to market

Mahmoud's friends have heard about Elizabeth, but not from Mahmoud. Abdelmajid's mother hears from her neighbour, Aisha, about the American girl, and of course she goes directly to her son for information. Abdelmajid is annoyed that he is hearing about Elizabeth from his mother rather than from Mahmoud himself, so he shrugs it off as if it is nothing. Now the mother, in her turn, interprets the shrug incorrectly; she fears that her son is protecting Mahmoud and therefore involved in a similar disgrace. So the mother spends the afternoon sitting next to her older son, Brahim, at the computer, trying to find out whether Abdelmajid is engaged in conversations with foreign women. But Brahim is not very helpful. Concerned that his mother will view his own search history or that he will accidently open a screen with iniquitous pictures, he spends the afternoon fumbling around the keyboard, his mother staring over his shoulder. She rebukes him, but it doesn't help: "You spend all day on that machine, and now you act as if you don't know how to operate it!"

Mahmoud has two best friends. One is Abdelmajid, and the other is Najib. When Mahmoud is away in Tamri, these two are often together, so when Mahmoud comes to town, they gather for an evening coffee and to share the latest local gossip. This afternoon, as most afternoons, they are headed to market to fulfil their mother's requests, and they have invited Mahmoud to join them. First for a bit of coffee, and then to the market to buy the things their mothers need for dinner. On this particular day, they are determined to gain more information about Mahmoud than their mothers have.

Mahmoud arrives at the café soaking wet; the rain has been pouring for days. "It's raining cats and dogs," he shouts in Arabic as he runs to embrace his friends. Abdelmajid laughs, while Najib looks annoyed. Najib knows this is typical of Mahmoud – directly translating American idioms to Arabic to show how clever he is, to separate between those who know enough English to laugh at his jokes and those who do not.

Mahmoud doesn't offer any information about Elizabeth until they ask him directly: "We heard about your American visitor, Mahmoud. Why aren't you introducing us to her?"

Mahmoud plays coy: "Oh, Elizabeth. She's an artist from New York."

"Well?"

"Well, she's here, and she's staying with my parents. What else do you want to know?"

"Why didn't you tell us about her?"

"Would I tell two cormorants how to steal my fish? She's in my house, and she's reading a book. She's smart and funny, and she's very nice." Abdelmajid and Najib notice that Mahmoud doesn't mention whether or not Elizabeth is pretty, so they draw their own conclusions with a wink to one another and lose interest in the conversation. They finish their coffee and get ready to leave the café.

When the three friends arrive at market, the afternoon crowds are loud and thick. They buy a few items to please their mothers: some fruits and vegetables, a few kilos of beans. They greet the vendors they know – some of whom were their classmates just a few years back. They wink and laugh as they hear a friend bargaining with two German tourists in incompatible versions of French.

When the friends walk past the fabrics of an upholstery shop, they see Zahra and her parents. Zahra, as everyone knows, has long held the attention and admiration of Mahmoud. She is his everlasting, and unattainable, object of desire. Zahra has never returned any of Mahmoud's overtures towards her, but this never daunts Mahmoud in his quest for her devotion. Mahmoud nudges his friends to follow and scuttles into Zahra's path.

They greet Zahra's parents first, while Zahra seeks a way around and past them. Her parents are too polite to take a quick exit, however, and Zahra knows she is stuck. Zahra's parents certainly do not share their daughter's distaste for Mahmoud: quite the opposite. They like his parents very much, and they believe everything they hear about Mahmoud: that he is intelligent, dedicated to his work, and fluent in English and French. The current gossip about Elizabeth has not yet reached their ears, and they have never read any of the poetry that Mahmoud has written to parody Abu Nawas. Therefore, they like him, and they believe he has a great future ahead of him.

"I thought you would be in Ifrane!" says Mahmoud to Zahra. This statement is untrue: he knows exactly where Zahra will be and when. He follows her movements as closely as possible through her cousins.

"I'm home for a weekend break."

"Are you graduating soon? How are your studies?" These questions are superfluous and disingenuous, but Mahmoud asks to impress Zahra's parents. Mahmoud knows very well that Zahra graduates this month, and he knows all about her master's degree in supply chain management. In fact, he can barely control his grief over her choice of major. Why would she study at the most prestigious university in Morocco and not take up a discipline worthy of her intellect and beauty? It irritates him. Zahra should be studying philosophy and literature, he thinks, something that would contribute to their future discussions as a couple.

Of course, he knows about her upcoming graduation. The whole city knows of Zahra's successful studies at the royal university, and no one is more jealous than Mahmoud, who knows every detail of the campus by studying its website. He is especially familiar with its elegant and well-appointed library, and he accurately assumes that Zahra has not even begun to plumb the depths of its collection in her three years of study.

As Mahmoud laments her wasted opportunities, Zahra secretly exults in the news that she is about to share with her parents at dinner: Renault Motors has offered her a coveted position in their corporate office in Rabat. She will receive a generous salary and a luxury apartment near her office. Because of her preoccupation with this news and her internal dialogue about how to present this offer to her parents, Zahra completely misses the discussion of her parents with Mahmoud. When she realises that her parents are inviting Mahmoud to her graduation in Ifrane, it is too late. She knows they are only being polite, and they don't expect him to accept, but she also knows, without the smallest doubt, that Mahmoud would crawl on his hands and knees from Essouaira to Ifrane for the privilege of attending the ceremony. She knows that he has no shame: he will spend the day sneaking into conversations with her professors and insinuating a closer connection with Zahra than is true.

Zahra is absolutely right. Mahmoud is already working on his plan for attending her graduation. He knows he can leave Elizabeth with his family. Even if his sisters are unkind and unpleasant with him, and even if they complain, he can count on their hospitality towards

Elizabeth. She would be well cared for in his absence. Mahmoud mulls his options, his mind full of questions and details. He considers his friends in Rabat and Casablanca, where he can spend the night in someone's cushioned salon without a hassle. As he walks towards his house, he detours to pass the bus station for a quick look at the schedule. He will need a bus to Marrakesh on Friday afternoon, then a train to Rabat or Casablanca. He'll arrive after midnight, sleep a little, then take an early train to Meknes, where he can get a grand taxi to Ifrane. By bus, train, and taxi, the trip will take two days, and he'll be lucky to arrive at the graduation on time. After the ceremony, he'll travel without any stops back to Essouaira.

His chief concern is money. He won't need a lot, but he needs enough for tickets. He tries to think of a way to convince Elizabeth to finance his trip without becoming suspicious. He will tell her that an uncle is dying, and his final wish is to see Mahmoud once more. He feels a bit guilty and uneasy about leaving Elizabeth behind with his family. He relies upon one single comforting thought: Elizabeth cannot communicate without him, and no embarrassing information can pass between Elizabeth and his family members.

Upon entering the house, however, he hears something that devastates his plans: French! He hears the women of the house – his mother, Naima, Fatiha, and yes, even Elizabeth – all speaking French and laughing together. Doom is a slap in his face.

Still alone in the front entry of the house and pale with dread, Mahmoud sits quietly on a bench to listen. Elizabeth has betrayed him with a secret weapon. He hears their laughter as the beating of a drum, a clock ticking away his moments until all hope is lost. Her father is Canadian! Mahmoud should have known. At least he should have asked. This miscalculation could cost him the trip to Zahra's graduation, to the dreamscape of Ifrane and its gem of a university.

But no, it can't be. Mahmoud is a resourceful man, and he will find a way. Now the four women chattering in the kitchen are his adversaries: they are obstacles to overcome. As he listens, their laughter becomes a cackling of hens. Mahmoud jumps up from the bench, strutting like a rooster into the kitchen, expecting to run them off, to scatter them to the four winds like frightened, flightless birds. Instead, he finds them inviolable, unified against him.

Here they sit together, enjoying one another's company and chatting like old friends. They scarcely notice Mahmoud, and when they do, they hardly give a nod in his direction. No one offers him tea, so he grabs a cookie from the middle of the table and skulks off, no longer a rooster, but a rat instead.

His plan is ruined. He can't leave Elizabeth behind to tell his family of the secrets she knows and to learn of the secrets his sisters hold against him. The dying uncle story won't work either, as no one in his family will collude. He imagines his sisters recounting his many failings and foibles, and Elizabeth asking prying questions to learn all she should not know.

Once in a while, Mahmoud gets caught in his own web of lies, and these are moments that challenge him intellectually. He doesn't mind. He simply finds the best way out. At the moment, he wishes that he had not brought Elizabeth to his family home. She should have remained a secret. He wishes that her visit did not coincide with Zahra's graduation. But what can he do? These are only details, minor problems to solve.

He considers other places to send Elizabeth in his absence, but no matter where he sends her, he cannot avoid the fact that she speaks French and can therefore reveal him to others. The only option, he thinks, is to convince her to go somewhere, perhaps Rabat, to stay in a hotel. She will have to wait for him alone. Mahmoud sends a text to a friend in Casablanca and to another in Rabat, asking about cheap accommodation. The friend in Rabat responds first with a suggestion. The price is 400 dirhams, a full month of rent for Mahmoud, but the cost must be borne by Elizabeth.

That night, as he drifts off to sleep, his thoughts wander between how to convince Elizabeth and how to impress Zahra. He imagines himself at Zahra's graduation, talking philosophy with her professors, dropping names like Sartre and even Badiou.

Secrets and public confessions

As Susan and Daoud travel from Kelaat M'Gouna to Fez one afternoon, it is still early in their relationship. They have allowed themselves to admit that they are fond of one another but are still cautious and politely distant.

```
July, 1990
```

```
Is this what it is supposed to be like?
How am I supposed to feel right now?
This protracted and awkward time of
getting    to    know    one    another,
negotiating the proper distances,
approaching and retreating while never
lapsing in my attention towards the
object of my fascination?
```

Daoud and Susan proceed carefully due to various factors: their student–teacher relationship, their sense of home and community, their concern for the emotional well-being of one another. It is a time of rich and interesting dialogues, an undertone of optimism, and a pleasant concord with one another.

During this time, Daoud makes several of these unusual invitations to Susan to travel to Fez with him. Susan isn't fully aware of how strange it seems to others – an unmarried man and woman travelling together over long distances. Daoud is keenly aware, of course, and so he makes these invitations with apprehension. He knows the consequences for Susan's reputation with his neighbours and relatives. He knows they will judge Susan harshly, and him too. He takes steps to mitigate the problem, and his parents, who genuinely like Susan, remind their neighbours that Americans are a little different: they spread the word about her impeccable behaviour and her close friendship with Amal. Once Susan and Daoud arrive in Fez, Daoud always invites a chaperone to accompany them, but of course these many precautions are not quite adequate, and some of the neighbours are troubled. As they say, Susan and Daoud spend quite a bit of time alone in the car, and no one can say for certain what happens between them in those hours.

Because of gossip in their early courtship, Daoud's neighbours and relatives have always been a bit sceptical of Susan. When she fasts during Ramadan, there are some who doubt her sincerity. To add to the complications, Daoud is considered a very good catch among his family's social circle, and there are a good number of young women who are disappointed and jealous when Susan arrives on the scene.

Yet in spite of these difficulties, Daoud likes to take Susan to Fez when they have an opportunity, where the lifestyle is more genteel, and the urban environment affords certain luxuries not available in Kelaat M'Gouna – hot running water, for example, and laundry machines.

On one of their trips, as Daoud and Susan explore safe topics of discussion, nothing too personal, they settle on a philosophy of siblings. Susan, who was raised in a culture that expects and even rewards sibling rivalry, being a place of intense competition and individualism, considers her sister a difficulty and a nuisance. Susan has a theory about siblings and cousins: she believes that cousins are much better, as their distance allows for some breathing room. She once heard her aunt regaling the younger children with heroic stories of their older sibling. None of these stories bothered Susan, who was free to admire this cousin or not, but the siblings feigned boredom in an effort to retreat from their mother's overzealous expectations.

American parents often seem determined to exacerbate sibling rivalry, perhaps in a misguided attempt at motivation. Sometimes becoming a younger sibling is like entering a beauty contest with mud on one's face – there really is no point in competing, and the child would much rather stay in the mud. Susan has a younger sister who responds to Susan's success with spectacular displays of lethargy. Their lives operate in an inverse proportion of success and failure.

"Don't you see, Daoud," Susan says, as a glorious lake appears in the desert. It is the lake named for Hassan Addakhil, just north of Errachidia, and its palm trees dance in the water, beckoning them like sirens. But they continue driving, anxious to be in Fez again. "Siblings are too close, and bound to detest one another."

But Daoud disagrees. He has many cousins, and they have always been his closest friends. The older boys taught him to play soccer and challenged him to play well. The girls would often flirt with him and tease him about marriage. He's glad that his parents don't expect him to marry one of his cousins, but that doesn't mean that he's free of speculation about it.

But there is none of that social pressure when it comes to his sister, Amal. She is almost twenty-six and still unmarried, so it seems she may remain unmarried and therefore his responsibility. It's not that she didn't have suitors. She did. Several men approached her family for Amal's hand. She accepted one and planned to marry him, but during the time of planning this wedding, she discovered him in a lie, an unnecessary lie about his whereabouts during Friday prayers. The lie may have seemed petty to some, but it mattered a great deal to Amal. After cancelling the wedding, she climbed the stairs to the second floor and entered a room that she rarely used, her bedroom, and there she stayed for some days, receiving only her mother with food and water, and allowing her mother to stay with her for an hour or so each day. She went through the books in her room, the books that she had kept since high school, and she read them again. When she returned to the first floor, she went back to sleeping on the cushions along the wall of the salon like the others, and no one said another word about a wedding for Amal.

Amal is a model Muslim - really a model human being, let's be honest. It's intimidating, but at the same time inspiring. Her life is devoted to the Qur'an as she herself understands it, and for her this means a life of service to the care and treatment of others. It's what I'm supposed to be doing as a Peace Corps volunteer, but it's Amal who does it with a full and willing heart. Besides her service to others, she never fails in her daily prayers, and she knows every word of the Qur'an by heart. She fasts often and brings food to the mosque each Friday so that the Imam can feed the hungry.

Last week I told Daoud that I miss certain foods from home. I wanted to eat Gouda and whole wheat bread; I wanted broccoli and strawberries. Daoud took me to a grocery meant for tourists, with ridiculously high prices. Thrilled, I picked out my groceries, and I couldn't wait to share them with Daoud's family. I thought I would cook a special meal for them, after how many meals they have made for me. But Amal won't eat these foods; she cannot bear to eat such expensive things. It feels wrong to her. I felt scolded, and my pleasure in the foods was diminished. I ate some alone with Daoud, feeling guilty. Later in the day, I saw that Amal was serving the leftovers to the plumbers and tile workers who had come to fix the bathroom. "But Amal wouldn't eat this food herself," I grumble crossly to Daoud, feeling Amal's perfection sharpening against my own poverty of spirit. I'm annoyed with everyone, including myself, but Daoud explains: "We must serve everyone, no matter who it is, as we would serve the most honoured guest. Think of it this way: Amal must consider your food to be the very best in the house at the moment."

Susan sometimes feels tense and anxious with Amal, knowing she can never measure up adequately to Amal's purity and steadfast piety. Yet Amal adores Susan as the sister she has always wished for. When Susan decides to open her arms to Amal, she discovers that her affection is reciprocated with unrestrained joy.

What Zahra tells

Zahra has imagined her graduation day many times. The vivid green lawns, where hundreds of important people gather to celebrate: ambassadors, palace representatives, CEOs from the Gulf, from Europe, from North America, any one of whom could offer a lucrative contract to a graduate. The prestige of the university is what attracts these students. Her professors attended Oxford, Harvard, and the Sorbonne, and Zahra has attended classes with a princess – a girl she now considers a friend. Her graduation is her opportunity to thank her parents and to share with them all this richness, to shine in her own light: but now Mahmoud is coming to ruin everything.

Zahra knows beyond a doubt that he will attend the graduation. He has been scheming for this invitation for three years. If he has to kill a pig and eat it, or otherwise mortgage his sick, hungry soul, he will do it – anything to be present on her lovely, shining, precious campus. Now Zahra considers withdrawing from the ceremony – not to be petulant or melodramatic but for valid concerns. She feels Mahmoud could easily say something to ruin her career.

"Why would father invite him, Mama, why?"

"Zahra, don't be silly."

"Mama, I'm not silly. I spent three years to earn this master's degree. It's my graduation, and now Mahmoud will ruin this day for me."

"The university is many hours from here, Zahra. Mahmoud will not be able to travel so far to attend."

"You don't know Mahmoud as I do, mother. I can guarantee that he will be there, and first in line for the best seat."

"Zahra, be reasonable. He has his teaching job. He can't possibly go all the way to Ifrane for your graduation. Your father merely invited him to be polite."

"Oh, my dear mother. You don't comprehend this man, Mahmoud. He has been waiting all his life for an invitation like this. He will sidle up to everyone – the president, the governing board, professors... He will convince everyone that we are his family, or worse... that I am engaged to marry him! He will find the directors of Maroc Telecom or the Royal Bank of Maghreb and start negotiating a salary. I promise you, Mama, he will ingratiate himself to every man in a proper suit."

"Zahra, I'm sorry, but it can't be helped. We invited him as a friend of our family. If he happens to come, which I doubt very much, we will treat him as an honoured guest. If it helps, I will tell your father to keep him close to us."

"I don't know if I want to keep an eye on him or keep a distance, Mama. Either way, he could say something to ruin me. I really can't believe we are in this dilemma."

"Zahra..."

"He will embarrass our entire family. I suppose you haven't heard about the American whore he is keeping in his mother's house."

"What? Zahra, what language! Is this what they teach you at that fancy school?

"Mama..."

"Zahra, what are you talking about?"

"Maybe you should ask Aunt Aisha. She can tell you everything about it. Mahmoud is not the man you think he is. I know his parents are good and kind, but this Mahmoud is a big problem. I hope you can find a way to keep him from my graduation. I really do."

"Zahra!"

"I will leave this decision to you and my father. I know you trust his family. But please ask my aunt and find out what devious tricks Mahmoud is planning. I need to finish some work on my thesis. I hope you don't mind."

With this, Zahra takes leave of her mother, who hurriedly pulls a jellabiya over her house clothes and wraps a scarf around her. She rushes off to her sister's house to find out whatever may be known about Mahmoud and his unimagined visitor.

Zahra is normally a gracious host, but she loses her sense of hospitality when Mahmoud is involved. She simply cannot bear the prospect of his marching around with his own sense of purpose on her special day: basking in her sunlight, breathing in the beauty of Ifrane.

Zahra imagines Mahmoud creeping up to her professors, the liar, to say how proud he is to have coached and mentored her. With his vague pronouncements and insinuations, he will take credit for each of her accomplishments.

Mahmoud is clever – there is no question of that – but he has nothing whatsoever to do with Zahra's studies. Even with his many attempts to talk with her, to ingratiate himself to her, she has hardly spoken two words to him since high school, and she feels even two words have been too many.

Of course, she knows exactly how Mahmoud feels about her choice of major, and she absolutely does not care. He can wave that theory book under her nose as much as he wishes, but she will never ask him about it. She can buy herself a whole library of literary theory after she announces the news of her contract with Renault and convinces her parents to let her sign. She can read volumes of poetry and literature every evening after her well-paid day at work. She can buy books and CDs and new clothes – but this will be her decision only and nothing to do with Mahmoud.

"My sister Aisha! What do you know about your neighbour's son?" Zahra's mother is anxious but still hopeful that Zahra has exaggerated Mahmoud's indiscretions.

"Do you mean Mahmoud? He arrived yesterday from Agadir with an American girl." Aisha always goes straight to the point.

"From Agadir? Is she a teacher like him?" She is still hopeful, still wanting to believe in Mahmoud's inherent goodness.

"I don't know – maybe. She's an artist. She speaks French and English."

"Really?"

"Her father is French, I think," says Aisha. "She's not very pretty, poor thing. Fatiha says he keeps the girl at home – going off with his friends and leaving the girl alone with her book and drawings."

"Why is she here?" Now Zahra's mother begins to understand her daughter's anxiety.

"No one knows. She came here alone to visit Mahmoud. You know these American girls. No one takes care of them. They travel alone as if they have no family or friends."

"Ay! I wish I had known. We saw him at market with his friends. Please don't tell anyone, because we like his family very much, but Zahra is angry. Mahmoud offered to attend her graduation. We invited him – just to be polite. We didn't think he would actually come, but he always asks about her, and he seems interested in her studies. Now Zahra is furious. She says we are ruining her graduation."

"Well, it doesn't matter. He won't be able to go." Aisha's certainty about this is soothing.

"Don't you think so? That's what I said, but Zahra believes he will be there."

"Well, he has his job, and now this guest. He'll be too busy. I don't see how he would be able to go to Ifrane. Tell Zahra not to worry. By the way, can you all come for dinner tomorrow? I want to make a special meal to celebrate Zahra's graduation."

"Yes, of course. Thank you."

"My dear niece, Zahra! Just yesterday she was a little baby learning to talk, and now look at her! She will soon have a master's degree! I heard she had a job in Rabat. Is it a good contract?"

"Rabat! No. Where would you get such an idea? No, Aisha, she won't live so far away. Her father will soon find something for her here. He is talking with his business contacts in the area, and I'm sure he will find a very good job for her. We want her job to be worthy of her education, of course, with a good salary, but her father will never permit her to live far away from us again. He is so proud to bring her back home with a master's degree."

Glamour and dust

When we first planned to travel to Casablanca, I imagined a glamorous modern city. Not that I expected to find Bergman and Bogart in trench coats, walking hand in hand in the fog – nothing quite so naïve – but certainly tree-lined boulevards, busy markets with colourful fabrics, and lovely modern buildings with flourishes of art deco. To my surprise, my beloved urges that we avoid Casablanca, board a train immediately, and go on to safer places. There is nothing glamorous about this city, he tells me, forget your Hollywood notions.

For Americans like me, Casablanca evokes an image of Humphrey Bogart bending forcefully over the helpless and delicate Ingrid Bergman, eternally preparing to kiss her. The space between them is a space of desire, of the *almost*. It resembles other romances – the powerful seduction by someone wealthy and enamoured who claims he cannot do without her, until the inevitable moment when he can, and she is left alone and drifting. It may be nation-to-nation or lover-to-lover – the dynamic is the same. When the powerful one feels desire, he doesn't care whether it will fade: he must have what he desires at the moment he desires it; then he must be able to dispose of it when it no longer suits him.

For years, the citizens of Morocco paid a tax to finance the mosque of Hassan II, an example of power bending the powerless. This mosque, with the tallest minaret in the world, reaches out from Casablanca into the

Atlantic Ocean. It is touted as the pride of its citizens, but there are many who resent its name, its opulence, and its cost.

If you want crumbling Hollywood visions, don't go to Casablanca: go instead to Agdz.

On our way to Agdz, driving treacherous mountain passes towards Zagura, we join for some time an assembly of elderly Portuguese daredevils in stock cars: two dozen couples driving in caravan, revving their engines like anxious NASCAR racers. We join their caravan because there is no way around them. They refuse to be passed, staying tightly in formation, and the road is unpredictable. In Agdz, they stop at the main intersection, where a line of restaurants seems welcoming. But the welcome is overly boisterous, with swarms of flies greeting us at the entrance. We know this routine too well: as soon as we order food, they will call all their cousins to the feast. We have often eaten our meals with these persistent divers, so that one hand is engaged in eating while the other flaps frantically and futilely. Today we wish to eat in peace, in an airtight restaurant with air conditioning. We leave the audacious road warriors and move along in search of a more relaxing environment.

At a pizzeria nearby, the employees all wear soccer jerseys and gather around a small screen to watch Barcelona play Madrid. Our request for pizza is waved off. "We can't turn on the oven," they say, "We don't know how, and the boss is out of town. Only the boss can make pizza. Very sorry." Sceptical, starving, and discouraged, we wander towards our car, and now we find good luck in the most unlikely of characters: a drunken, stumbling man approaches with advice. His father-in-law's restaurant is the best in town, he says. He would take us, but his father-in-law would be furious to see him inebriated. He points us in the right direction, and we go. We can never be too certain of our sources, but we soon discover that our guide has directed us towards a rare find.

Elaborate tile work covers every surface of this opulent palace: now in shades of grey, unfortunately, instead of the spectacular bright blues of its past. A labyrinth of banquet tables spreads throughout the main floor, in typical Moroccan fashion with cushioned benches. The low backrests allow patrons to see all the others and interact across the space. We can imagine lavish dinner parties for hundreds of stylish guests.

Several fountains line the entry and main hall, and twin swimming pools sparkle from the back. We imagine Rock Hudson and Marilyn Monroe lounging and laughing at poolside as waiters arrange elaborate dishes of fruits and juices around the deck for their entourage.

The place is empty, except for us and the father-in-law of our guide. There are tiles missing here and there, and the fabrics are worn. But still it evokes the Hollywood version of Morocco I had expected. The elegant main floor could easily transform into a smoky dance hall, with a man at the piano, and a lovely mysterious woman – displaced in a foreign land. Then imagine the piano replaced by a full orchestra and another woman in a slinky dress at the microphone. The ghosts of the past light the candles on the chandeliers, crystal glasses clink, and dancers float on smoky air.

Over the span of decades, the hotel has degenerated into shades of dust and grey, and the place has lost its clientele. Perhaps the ghosts could tell us more about the mysterious town of Agdz: we have heard of secret prisons and torture. What really happened here in Agdz? What would the silenced voices tell? Where was the prison, and what happened to its occupants? We are curious about this post-glamorous town. Are the secrets permanently buried or yet striving to the surface?

Susan and Daoud: between a rock and a hard place

July, 1990

First of all, I must note that I have never experienced such heat as this day in July, and I dread the months to come. Everyone says that these flapping robes and scarves are meant to help with the heat, to create some sort of air circulation; this is not true, as far as I can tell. To me, these are just layers of fabric, like I would wear in the coldest days of winter, and I long for a day at the beach, a scanty swimsuit, a cold glass of water, a splash of whiskey or rum. I'm tired of all this piety and abstinence, honestly, this desert, this grinding poverty of dust and rickety bicycles.

This morning I meet a woman as I walk towards the language institute, dressed like every other grown woman in voluminous folds of black cloth. Only her eyes, her frightened young eyes, peek out from the fabric. At first, I

131

feel bumped and jostled – I move to balance and steady myself – then I feel papers pushed into my palm. Afraid, I clench the papers in my fist, not changing my glance to look back at the woman nor down at the papers in my own hand. Now I'm trembling, and for good reason.

At the language institute, students are beginning to arrive in the lobby for their morning coffee and croissants. I walk past them, anxious and breathless, to Daoud's classroom, where he sits alone preparing for his classes. I whisper what happened. I hand the notes over. I'm anxious about my boldness – no one has ever seen me alone with Daoud before, and I don't want my classmates to see us.

As Daoud reads the first note, his expression changes from curious to disbelieving to concerned. He explains that the note comes from an activist group trying to bring attention to the children in prison in Kelaat M'Gouna, Agdz, Laayoune, and Tazmamart. The first note is typed and formal. The group explains who the political prisoners are and what they are accused of: some are accused of betraying King Hassan II, others advocate for Western Saharan independence. The children are suffering for their parent's sins, even though some of the parents are deceased. The second paper is written in a child's hand. It has a simple message: "Please stop them from killing us. My brothers and sisters are together here. Please." The third is also handwritten. It pleads with me directly, calling me by name, to contact as many foreign journalists as I possibly can with this information.

So now, we're afraid, both of us, but we know we have to do something. We will, but this puts us all in danger. We have to proceed with caution. Daoud wants to talk to his parents first, which is frustrating to me, but I understand.

Susan is afraid but ready to help, and Daoud feels the same. They want to do what is right, and they intend to, but their resolve does not change the fact that they are both in grave danger.

"I will talk with my parents, Suzy. Wait a few days so that we can take care of this together."

But Daoud's discussion with his mother is surprisingly vehement: "Daoud, please leave this issue alone. This is not our affair! Daoud, you are so young. You have to learn the reality about living in this country!"

"Mama! Don't be silly! This is my country also, since my birth. Certainly I know how to live here."

"You are talking about involving an American in the country's internal affairs. The authorities will not stand for it. You should know this if you know your country well. I mean it. If you care for Susan, you cannot be involved in this trouble with the prisoners. You need to leave this problem, Daoud, or it will become your family's problem also. You cannot involve yourself, your family, and especially your American friend. Think of what might happen to her, or to your sister."

"We aren't involved, Mama." Daoud is whispering now, even in the home of his parents, he feels a need to whisper. He feels strangely weak. "Susan received these notes. I assume they chose an American on purpose. They want her to send the papers to an American journalist."

"You cannot allow this!"

"Mama. She has a friend from college, a reporter. Susan won't be identified. She will send the envelope without her name, and then she will call her friend to assure that the letter has arrived. That's all."

"It's a terrible risk, Daoud. I don't have to tell you this: the authorities don't take these things lightly. And I don't have to tell you this either: our king is Hassan the Second, the leader of the faithful – a gift to us from God – descendant of the Prophet, peace be upon him. It is not our place to criticise."

"Mama, there are children being held in these prisons. Is this the will of God?"

Now Daoud's mother breaks down in tears. "I know, Daoud; I know everything about it, but I am very frightened for you and Susan. Please be careful. We love you, and we love Susan, too. We can't lose you, and you can't allow anything to happen to her. Think of her parents! What would happen if you and Susan end up in one of these horrible prisons, Daoud?"

Daoud pauses for a moment. His mother's fears are justified. Hassan II has been in power since 1961, and now, thirty years later, he is popular, known for his wit and charm, always elegant in photographs with the kings and queens, presidents and prime ministers of the world. Moroccans are proud of his projects – highways, trains, buildings, universities, even entire cities. Agadir was devastated after the earthquake, and is now a thriving modern jewel of a city.

Even Daoud admires the king's academic prowess and inspiring speeches, his ability to garner respect and lead with authority, but this powerful leadership style comes with some caveats: his authority cannot be questioned, and his methods of silencing his enemies and critics are often cruel. The children are in prison because their father tried to depose their king. What will happen to Susan if Daoud acts imprudently?

"Mama, I really do understand your point. I don't know the best course of action, but we can't turn our eyes away from this suffering. Susan was approached directly, by name. She won't be persuaded to ignore this issue now that it has come to her attention. Besides, Mama, you know that we can't ignore injustice. The Prophet, peace be upon him, has taught us very clearly on this point. He would give anything to help others – his own food, his own clothing, anything that another person needed. He gave everything he had, and he didn't care about the consequences. Mama, this is one of those moments that will be recorded by the angels, and we have to face it in the right way. This is how we learn what kind of people we are, what we deserve on our Judgement Day."

Susan and Daoud are not the only ones to receive notes like these from brave, thoughtful, quiet activists, and who knows how the story travels? At some point, the story breaks in the French newspapers, and the royal palace moves quickly to change its position. Soon the prisoners are released, and not only that. The release of these prisoners will be followed by a series of democratising reforms that King Hassan II declares through the 1990s and until his death in 1999, including the release of hundreds of political prisoners, an empowered Royal

Council for Human Rights, and shared governance with the opposition party.

A year later, the release of the Kelaat M'Gouna prisoners is meant to be a quiet event, but word travels fast, and the entire village arrives to serve as unofficial witnesses. They see the prisoners emerge, some blinking in the light, some crying, some crawling. Susan feels weak. She fights the urge to vomit, but her stomach aches with it. Daoud, hesitant, puts his hand under Susan's elbow, afraid she might faint, and worried he might not have his usual strength in the face of this terrible moment. Susan is upset by her own response, and she appreciates Daoud's hand under her elbow. She breathes deeply to stabilise her balance.

Groups of prisoners emerge slowly – not only men but also women and their children – veiled women and girls who were provided with fresh jellabiyas just before their release. The prisoners move at different rhythms and tempos – some dodging furtively as if cowering before a weapon, others striding forward to meet the world in triumph. Each of the prisoners is small, thin, discoloured, and deformed. Some carry the guilt and betrayal of the unfairly treated, others the self-confidence of the falsely accused. The children have spent their formative years in prison. As they walk towards the bright hot day, they seem disoriented and frightened, ready to turn around and go back to their only familiar place.

The sight of these children shames Daoud. Faced with their anguish, he feels small, distressed, and lonely. He has been blind and deaf to this suffering, but even worse: once he learned of it, he lacked the ferocity to run shouting and cursing, beating against the prison's walls, making it crumble to the ground, exposing the truth inside. He could have done more.

While Daoud struggles with these feelings, Susan reels with anger and nausea. This event takes her back to the days of her childhood, when she followed every detail of the Iranian hostage crisis. Her friends think she is brave to be in Peace Corps, but she feels they are wrong. She looks at these broken people and wonders whether she herself could survive such conditions. What would she do, she wonders, if she were held against her will? She considers the possibility that she joined Peace Corps not out of bravery but out of cowardice, as some sort of cure, a way to face her frightened self.

In different ways, this moment takes Susan and Daoud to the edge of their own despair. The release of prisoners, an event they had anticipated as a source of elation, brings instead a private sense of failure, depravity, and self-loathing. They walk away together but quietly, a rare silence for these two, and years pass before they are able to share their feelings aloud to one another.

Never alone

A woman alone in Morocco will soon have a story to tell. Someone may approach her, question her, pursue her. Look around you on any Moroccan street: do you see anyone, man or woman, walking alone? It just isn't done. Moroccans prefer to be together, and they take time to accompany one another. Men often walk hand in hand or arms around the other. Women move together with their shoulders touching. Companions stay close – close enough for whispers. A woman alone is to be pitied, befriended, or abused.

I learn my lessons quickly. Once I step away from my group just to see a leather purse that has caught my eye in a market stall. It isn't that I mean to cause a ruckus, simply that I don't want to interrupt my beloved and his brother as they chat along in front of me. My miscalculated step back results in disaster: there is an insult I don't understand, and my beloved, whom I had assumed was too engrossed in discussion to notice, turns to assail the miscreant. There are shouts, more insults, a tumult and commotion. I wait anxiously for the argument to subside.

A woman alone in Morocco will not be alone for long. Someone will be her friend. If my beloved cannot accompany me, he finds someone well-trusted and reliable who can. Yet here is Elizabeth, alone and unsuspecting. This is what has worried us: Susan, Sophie, Sanaa, and me: that Mahmoud would fail to protect her, that she would wander alone and vulnerable. Mahmoud has left Elizabeth in Rabat while he pursues dreams that don't include her.

Perfectly clear

My beloved notices every movement of my face, and he reads each flicker to precision. Because he can do this, he can also make his own face implacable. I am not deterred, however: I have learned to read his shoulders and neck if his face is incomprehensible. In this way we carry on an invisible conversation, an intimacy that people notice without understanding. Since the day my beloved declared his love for me, he began to tell me everything: from the smallest detail to the largest. Even now, we narrate our life together as a continual whisper in the ear: Did you see that? What does it mean? That reminds me of... Remember when...

He tells me everything because he knows how it all interests me. This is something that is true for us that remains surprising to others. Thus have many been surprised to learn that everything they say about me, no matter the language, is known to me. Some people learn this fact through a series of embarrassing episodes. Their unkind words are translated to me directly, without nuance, without assuaging. My beloved wants me to know exactly what people say so that I am aware of everything happening around me. And I am keenly aware: sometimes to the point of distress. Let me explain.

In Morocco I have experienced a wide range of comments about me – from the warm and enthused to the shy and uncertain to the downright antagonistic. Since I became his intended, I have experienced the bitterest of commentary from my beloved's friend Abderrahim and his rude wife, Hoda.

My beloved once enjoyed his friendship with Abderrahim, but that was long ago, when they were students together at the university in Marrakesh. Abderrahim was never the brightest student, but he was diligent. He studied boring and technical topics and avoided philosophy, but it suited him, and he eventually earned a doctorate and a university teaching post. Then he made the unfortunate decision to marry one of his students. Couldn't he have waited until she had graduated before courting her? Couldn't he have waited, at least, until she had finished his class? He could have saved himself a great deal of trouble. My beloved considers his friend's hasty misjudgements to be quite grave, but he is not one to give unsolicited advice. When Abderrahim does eventually request some advice, it is the eve of the wedding: Abderrahim in a panic, and my beloved in no position to change the course of events. What is to be done in these awkward moments? An imminent wedding is not something to debate. My beloved simply wishes his friend the best and offers his prayers.

This unfortunate match turns disastrous: the wife is an irrational child, unable to reconcile her material desires with her financial circumstances. Why did she marry a teacher? Perhaps she had expected her husband's salary to be ample or perhaps she thought that the book he co-authored with his adviser on the influence of the 1960 earthquake on the immigration patterns around Agadir would become a bestseller. In either case, what a fool.

Problems exacerbate rapidly: Hoda's poor upbringing becomes the subject of hushed discussions among the faculty; her lack of tact is noted. Hoda complains about her husband's salary; she rails on about academic women who go in public unveiled; and she invents ridiculous stories about shopping in Paris. When it comes to topics of interest to historians and philosophers, of course, she has nothing to offer. The women of the faculty, having worked diligently enough, having published in journals prestigious enough, to withstand the sexist scrutiny of their male colleagues, have little patience for young male scholars with impetuous wives. Abderrahim and Hoda are quietly excluded from social events, and his prospects as a scholar are diminished. He knows this is happening but feels powerless to change it.

Hoda may fantasise about trips to Milan and Paris for her wardrobe development, but her husband cannot afford such luxuries. As it is, he takes on extra jobs at language schools until he is working twelve-hour days, with no time to write the necessary articles for his tenure. Hoda is envious and pouting, but there is nothing her husband can do to satisfy her, and his impotence causes a painful rift between them. Desperate to force her husband to spend more time and money on her, Hoda makes the same irrational decision as many other equally irrational women: she secretly stops taking her birth control pills. Soon pregnant and even more irritable than before, her bulging stomach only serves to deepen the gap between them. Abderrahim despairs of his marriage and becomes cold and sarcastic, as neither his love nor his efforts bring joy to her.

On a certain evening I face Hoda, and my beloved stands behind me, also facing her. We are trying to leave their home, and we have been aiming for the door, but she has long detained us by her steady chatter. Suddenly, I realise that Hoda, who assumes that I cannot understand her in Moroccan Arabic, is offering herself to my beloved. Her husband will be going away for a few days, she says, and will be leaving some space in her bed! With effort, I keep an impassive look on my face, pretending not to understand, when Abderrahim appears, and his wife chokes on a sentence. My beloved asks Hoda to repeat herself, as if confused by her meaning. Abderrahim doesn't allow it, though, and I wonder whether he is protecting his wife or himself from an unknown but inevitable truth. Soon we are released from the relentless sound of Hoda's voice, and we leave, bemused and speculating on the truth between those walls.

Abderrahim and Hoda sometimes distract themselves from their miserable marriage by focusing instead on how much they dislike me. For them, I am an obstacle blocking their way to full communion with my beloved. Imagine Hoda, gossiping and complaining about my uncovered head. Imagine how they criticise me to my beloved, focusing on my faults, both real and imagined. After my beloved rejects her advances, Hoda devises a new plan. She invites my beloved to dinner, alone of course, promising to invite several beautiful young women – friends and relatives of hers. Hoda considers my beloved a very good catch who is wasted on me.

What Abderrahim and Hoda never realise is how often we narrate them to one another. Because I cannot communicate clearly in their language, they consider me insignificant, illiterate, and incapable of rational thought. Not knowing how I narrate them, they act in unconscionable ways.

Should I care?

The point is that I am not one of God's angels taking notes: I'm just a mortal narrator. I have my faults and misinterpretations. If I appoint myself their narrator, this is their misfortune; they also narrate me, however, so I have my own troubles. We are fiction to one another. We are truth-once-removed; we live with our hearsays and imprecisions.

One weekend, my beloved and I traipse along the Mediterranean coast, where each little town is holding its summer festival. We drive from Tangier to Tétouan, to Martil and Nador. We cross the border to Spain's North African fortress of Melilla for Spanish paella by the sea. We visit El Hoceima's cliffs above the water and the lapping waves at Saadia's beaches. It is the time of year when Moroccans living in Europe return to visit their families on the Rif, and flashy cars crowd the streets.

We play like children at these festivals, eating cotton candy, strolling near the sea, and telling the kinds of stories from our childhood that such settings evoke. My beloved tells of the day his parents searched desperately at the beach for him, fearing he had drowned, as he played soccer with new acquaintances far from the water's edge. I tell of dropping my cotton candy at the county fair and crying to see how much sand it picked up.

But in the midst of our playful holiday, my beloved takes a call from Abderrahim and tells him about our travels. Within a day they appear in the town, determined to join our holiday and find a wedge to shove between us. And this time they are almost successful because I'm pretty angry when they arrive. Not only this: Hoda is determined to have this holiday at my beloved's expense. Abderrahim and Hoda haven't any money, nor have they any shame. She orders expensive platters and desserts, and Abderrahim never fights for the bill as Moroccan tradition expects. After two days of this, I do as Moroccan tradition expects: no direct confrontation, just a simple excuse. "Oh, well, this has been a lovely vacation, and I'm so glad that you joined us for some time. We have to go to Spain on the ferry this afternoon." You see, it had to be another country because I was pretty sure that Hoda wouldn't have a passport. With any other lie, Hoda would have found a way to join us.

In spite of Hoda's bitterness, the Mediterranean coast is soothing. The gem of the world is this sea: a place to stay forever. Just think of the great works created near this sea, and no wonder. Who could live here uninspired? From the ancient masterpieces of Homer, da Vinci, and Ibn Rushd to the modern ones of Camus, Hemingway, Ben Jelloun, and countless others, the Mediterranean is fertile and nourishing, the source for some of the most creative works in history.

The people of the Mediterranean are the luckiest in the world, but like all lucky people, such as those who are loved, recognition of our good fortune comes and goes. When we are most lucky we may fail to notice, but when our luck passes the loss is acute. For that reason, we should look at our loved ones each day through a certain lens of awe and incredulity – not only because we love them but because of the grief that would follow the loss of them.

Susan's confession of faith

Susan's first experience with Ramadan is not easy, but she becomes attuned to the rhythm of it. There isn't food around, and so she fasts with the community, and the villagers quietly discuss her – is she fasting with us? Or is she eating in private to be polite?

Invitations come in shy whispers at first, but Susan is a gracious guest at iftar, and soon she receives more invitations to iftar celebrations than she can accept. It doesn't take long before she realises that the holy month is a joyful time, and she floats through the days without feeling much hunger.

March 1991

Thinking back to Georgetown, I remember attending one iftar dinner. Who invited me? I guess it was Abdi (I can't believe we called him "Abdi". Did he introduce himself that way? Or did someone else decide to call him that?) Anyway, it was a lovely dinner, and so moving. A simple ceremony first: brief prayer of thanks, small bite of food and drink of water, then a communal prayer before the feast. I wanted to join the women standing shoulder to shoulder then kneeling together, but as a non-Muslim

146

I could only watch and say a silent prayer of my own. It was probably some self-centred prayer about my grades. But anyway, the evening did help me understand some things. I became more aware of the Muslim students and their sacrifices during Ramadan. I realised I should eat privately during the month so as not to tempt anyone who might be fasting, and I tried to be considerate, knowing that many of the people in my Arabic and Middle-Eastern Studies courses might be weaker and less alert or energised than usual.

When I got the Peace Corps assignment, I knew that there would be fasting during Ramadan, of course, but I didn't realise how much it would affect my life. Ramadan in Morocco is nothing like Ramadan at Georgetown: everyone says I can eat whenever I want, but there's not any food around. The grocery, bakery, and cafés are all closed, and I'm not much of a cook myself, especially in this tiny room, and I don't want food in here because the next thing will be insects or rodents.

I'm thinking that I'll fast with everyone and become a full participant in Ramadan. Everyone else can do it, so why can't I? Besides, I'll have a full appreciation for what this place is all about.

In Morocco, Susan becomes enamoured with Islam. She admires the selflessness and kindness ingrained in Muslim thought, and she waits with anticipation to hear the muezzin call the faithful to their prayers. She glimpses fitfully, even enviously, into the mosques with their luxuriant, colourful rugs and ornate tiled walls and fountains, wishing she could enter.

When she begins asking her friends about the idea of converting to Islam, they treat her with a polite indifference that she interprets as discouragement. Her friends tell her, even Daoud tells her, and with great seriousness, not to convert unless she knows the Qur'an and Hadiths very well and feels certain she is prepared to follow them. They tell her that life in Islam is full of demands upon her time, her habits, and her beliefs. Sometimes they say it will be too much for her, that she will become tired of all the requirements.

But then their own love for Islam comes forth. She hears them discuss the joys of Islamic practices and principles, the beauty of one's life when following the path of God, the peace and serenity that such faith provides.

Raised in a protestant family, Susan never really questioned the existence of God, and she celebrated all the Christian holidays perfunctorily. Church was always there, in the background of her life, and God was a very distant star. As she slowly studies the Qur'an and prepares to convert to Islam, she wonders whether she will be welcomed as a Muslim or if she will always feel herself an outsider.

On the day set for her confession of faith at Friday prayers, Jumaah, she wakes at dawn when she hears the first call to prayer. She says a brief prayer then to the God she has always known – the same God she will proclaim today at the mosque. She prays for strength for the day, and she asks for God to guide her. She practises again the

Shahada that she has practised over the past several weeks, hoping not to make a mistake on the microphone later in the day.

> Until now, I've been alone in this
> world. Today is different – today I
> become part of a community larger than
> myself. Too excited to sleep, too early
> to rise. Tomorrow I will rise for prayer
> at this time, but not today. I don't
> yet know how to perform ablutions for
> prayer, but I will learn this morning
> from Amal.

Susan believes that this day will reveal all the secrets of Islam. She believes that she will learn how to pray. It isn't true. It will take years before Susan knows all the subtle aspects of her religion, but this will not diminish her early experiences as a Muslim nor cause any problems in the present. The subtleties will only enhance her life over time.

Finally she hears Amal at her door. Susan has everything she needs in a plastic bag: towel, hairbrush, small bottle of shampoo. At the public bath, the hammam, she listens to the sounds of a village's women waking up, discussing their world and its many burdens and requirements. She hears outcries of joy and grief. There are few private emotions in the village, and the small details of their world belong to everyone in it.

Today everyone wants to touch Susan, to reach out to her and hug her. As Amal tells the women about Susan's conversion, everyone wants to hear the story of why: how did she come to believe in the Prophet, peace be upon him, as the last prophet of God? They want her to articulate the details of her decision, and they want to celebrate with her. But Susan feels inadequate to explain why, and some of the story seems wrong to her. She tries her best. First the Qur'an: she was curious about a book that could change the world. Then the sights: the beauty of a minaret, a scholar engrossed in study. Next the sounds: calls to prayer, recitations. Later, the goodness and charity of Muslims, their commitments to one another, to social justice and self-sacrifice.

> People keep asking me what called me to Islam, and I can't really say. They want something specific, some phrase or some moment in time. I don't know. I can't even read Arabic very well, although I'm learning, and it moves me to tears. At first, I only knew the sound of the Qur'an, just the sound from the muezzin, the lovely sound of call to prayer. Now I'm becoming fully aware of the richness of the words given to the Prophet, and only now am I ready to declare in the mosque on Friday prayer the words that every Muslim declares: there is no God but God, and Mohammed is his Prophet.

Today Susan is warmed inside and out – by the heat of the baths, by the many kind words offered to her throughout the morning. When Susan and Amal arrive home from the bath, Susan finds a gift on her bed. Someone has laid out a beautiful new jellabiya, scarf, and slippers for her to wear. Smiling, weepy, she dresses herself, grateful for this family who has welcomed her and for the community around her. Susan feels that hundreds, perhaps thousands, will pray for her today, and she feels a rush of pleasure at this thought.

Indeed, everyone wants to be a part of Susan's special day. Everyone wants to touch her and welcome her to her new community of the faithful. If Susan once doubted that she would be accepted, she needn't have. Oh, a few jealous women will make comments that question her motives, but these voices will be few, relatively quiet, and quickly contradicted by kinder voices. God is merciful, they will say, gently reminding critics that it is sinful to question the faith of others. Believers should take care to refrain from judgements, and sins should be left for God alone to judge.

Later that day, she stands between Amal and Khadija, their shoulders pressed closely together. All of the women that Susan knows are close by. Amal has assured Susan that she only has to follow the others as they move through the prayers. Susan fears she may stand or rise too early, but when she feels all the women, so close and reassuring, she understands Amal's point: there is very little room for error. She will move when they move, in the way they move. All she must do is join them. As they listen, the words pour over Susan. She understands much of what the Imam says, and she is soothed by the musical tone of his voice. When it is time to pray, Susan does just as Daoud advised: she prays the prayers she remembers from her childhood: the 23rd and 51st Psalms of David. She only changes "create in me" to "create in us" because she feels so close to the others around her.

Then she feels Amal and Khadija squeezing her hands. She knows it is time for her confession of faith. The door to the chamber opens, and the Imam is there with a microphone. Susan feels her knees tremble. Khadija and Amal continue to hold Susan's hands as they walk towards the smiling Imam. At this moment, Susan cannot remember a single word of the confession she has been rehearsing for the past two weeks. The Imam says a few words of welcome to Susan, and then he nods to inquire whether she is ready. Susan nods back, and the Imam begins to guide her in the Shahada, a few words at a time: lā ʾilāha ʾillallāh, Muḥammad rasūlu-llāh. Silently, Susan reminds herself also in English: There is no God but God, and Muhammad is the messenger of God.

And then the Imam goes back to conclude the worship. Susan stands, tears streaming down her face, as she is welcomed with many hugs and caresses from the Muslimah sisters around her. As she exits with them, there is Daoud, with his father, smiling at Susan. Many crowds pass by on their way to their homes and businesses, curious to see the woman whose voice just proclaimed the faith they all share.

> The day passes by in a state of elation. Neighbours come to the house with gifts: scarves, slippers, an ornate copy of the Qur'an in English and Arabic, prayer beads. Many people pass through the doors this day, a day of celebration for everyone, it seems.

Susan's faith grows over the days and weeks, becoming a light and a comfort to her. Often she cries as she prays with her friends, so moved by the physical, emotional, and spiritual aspects of prayer.

There are aspects that challenge Susan, as the rhythm of her day changes. There are regimens to follow. She learns how to cover her head properly for prayer, how and when to perform ablutions. She finds herself the centre of several ongoing debates: some of the women think Susan should only pray in Arabic, while others argue she would pray more meaningfully in her native language, with maybe a preface in Arabic. Some argue about whether women must cover their heads in public, or only for prayer.

But this is a debate that goes on frequently, and it is not only about Susan.

> As a Muslim, Ramadan becomes a transcendent experience. When I first arrived in Morocco, Ramadan felt like a constant misery of hunger, but now I float peacefully through the days, hardly feeling it. I may be anxious for the evening to set in, but not for the feasting: rather for the recitation of the Qur'an that I long for each night, surrounded in the mosque by solemn and prayerful women, shoulder to shoulder, listening to the verses.

Daoud is surprised by how Susan embraces her Islam, and it creates within him a resurgence of childhood memories – learning to recite long passages of the Qur'an before he and his friends could start their soccer games in the late afternoon. Now the recitations become more meaningful for him, and as he answers Susan's many questions, he also becomes curious and searching about the meanings of certain passages in the Qur'an. He returns to the Qur'anic studies of his youth in an effort to anticipate Susan's wonderings. He marvels at the changes he sees in Susan and within himself as they pray together.

One of the things that he remembers from his childhood lessons is the importance of marriage in Islam, and he begins to consider his own desire to marry Susan. He hasn't mentioned it to anyone, but his prayers are increasingly centred around the question of marriage.

Daoud's friends begin to tease him about how devout he is becoming, but he finds, to his surprise, that the teasing doesn't bother him. He feels grateful to be moving within a path of grace, and his love and admiration for Susan grows. He narrows his gaze to see a glow around her: a joy greater than she knows that she is nevertheless responsible for creating.

Elizabeth in Rabat

Before dawn, Rabat is an ocean-side village, but when the sun rises, it becomes a large modern city again. Rabat is a place of possibility. It provokes the imagination, and potently. Here Elizabeth can allow her thoughts to wander from the current moment into something new.

She is lonely but undaunted, determined to create a special day for herself. She wakes just early enough to hear the sound of the sea. As she gazes out of her window, she views the city in its daily transformation, and she hears a dramatic shift – from the sound of waves breaking against the cliffs to the polyphony of the city: its traffic, its crowds, the sound of construction workers building a high-speed train.

Ready to witness a great city in action, Elizabeth quickly showers, dresses, and descends to the lobby of her hotel.

The mosque of the Almohad dynasty waits high above the city, waits for Elizabeth to walk among its gaps and open spaces. When the dynasty began to crumble in 1199 with the death of Sultan Yacoub al-Mansour, the building project also ceased. For eight hundred years, this mosque has waited for someone to come to prayer. Two hundred massive columns, each wider than the oldest tree, have never held a roof aloft. The mosque will never be decorated in intricate patterns of tile, never feel the weight of its thousands of worshippers kneeling together in prayer.

In these many centuries, this half-finished project, its partly constructed tower, half its intended height, has been soaring over the city of Rabat. What is this platform – its weight, its lightness? Why is it still reminding us of what could have been? How long will it reach towards the sea? A suggestion of greatness, a hope.

heArtblog, Sept 19

I have found a nice hotel in Rabat. Too expensive for my budget, but I don't care. I have a lot to think about, and I want comfort: a restaurant, a view of the ocean, fresh and cosy linens to nestle me.

Early in the morning, I ask the doorman to call a taxi, and I go first to the mosque, if I can call it that, of Sultan Yacoub al-Mansour. I can only imagine what this mosque wanted to be – grand and elegant, welcoming. But it has always been this – a series of lonely pillars, a light wind filled with the sea, an open space empty like a new canvas, pillars framing what could have been.

It's a space that moves me to tears, and I wonder how it might feel to enter a mosque for prayer. I imagine myself dressed in a veil, covered from head to toe in soft and flowing fabrics.

And suddenly serenity descends upon me, and for a moment I forget that I am

Elizabeth, left behind in Rabat by a man
who may or may not care about me, who
may or may not return for me. For a
moment, I have no identity, no relations,
no past, and no future. I am simply a being
– at peace with the wind and the sea. In this
way I walk along the beachfront below
Rabat's famous cliffs and ramparts, where
small boats chase one another on the
choppy surface of the sea.

Later, I wander through the old medina,
feeling at peace with myself. I find a small
bookshop, and something that I didn't
know I was looking for: a slim volume of
poetry in Arabic with side-by-side
translations in French. It is elegant and
beautiful, and I vow to myself that I will
hide it until I am certain of someone's love
and certain of my own.

Outside again, I breathe deeply, look out to
the sea, imagine the pirates of Salé on the
water, long ago. I consider for a moment
the life of a pirate – fearing sleep lest one
be thrown overboard at a vulnerable
moment.

In the late afternoon, I reach Moulay
Ismail's 17th-century palace, now the
Oudaya Museum. I wander through the
palace of the great sultan, among the
carpets and jewels, statues and sculptures;
I move among the flowers of his garden
and reach out to the cool waters of his

fountains. My art history major prepared me for a life like this – a life of colour and beauty.

And here I need a moment to really talk to myself. I have long believed that necessity – money – has forced me into a hack. I have longed for the patronage of someone like the great sultan, someone who could relieve me of my material concerns, allow me to do my work without sacrifice.

And here I stop myself because it isn't true. I am simply creating excuses. I imagine the patronage of a sultan, the constraints involved in pleasing his eye. It's not what I would want.

I know what to do as an artist, and I know how. What I haven't known is my capacity for passion, for love. I am learning about this now. I must look inside myself and face an uncomfortable fact: I have impeded my growth as an artist because of fear – a fear that is laden with lethargy and doubt. But if my life is to have any meaning, I must know my own talent, and I must work. Here, in Moulay Ismail's garden, I respond to a necessary impulse: to cast off my material concerns and become the artist I have wanted to be.

A wedding, a marriage

In Morocco, weddings happen quickly. Once the families have agreed, there is no reason to wait very long. Within months, the dresses and equipment are rented, food arranged, musicians hired, and the guests begin converging for the celebration. Islam emphasises the spiritual aspects of marriage, based not on passionate embraces and feelings but on the family's desire to do God's will and bring happiness to the community. Marriage provides companionship: a partner who brings you closer to your own goodness and to God's will for humans on earth. Family members and friends from all over the country make donations of clothing, decorations, and food – always to show love for the marriage and to knit one another ever closer together.

At first this marriage is a disappointment to Khadija, whose cousin's daughter was always meant to be Daoud's wife. Indeed, this young woman, a kind-hearted, intelligent, and diligent worker, having long understood herself to be Daoud's intended, had left herself without other options. Daoud's decision to marry Susan creates quite a bit of dissonance among the cousins until Umar takes the lead, sparing Daoud from several awkward discussions.

Unaware of the politics, Susan begins to experience what it means to marry not just a man, but an entire community. She is surprised when the women come to her with a prenuptial agreement, according to the

requirements of the Qur'an. This is meant to protect Susan
from any hardships in the future, but she wants to refuse
it, wants to say that it is a pessimistic way to begin a
marriage. When she tells her parents, they are impressed
with this aspect of Islam, the idea that a woman should
have her property rights and finances protected whether
or not the marriage is successful. They tell her not to think
too much about it, just to sign the paper and forget it.

This is how it begins: when Daoud first decides to
propose marriage to Susan, he discusses it first with his
father; then together, they approach his mother for her
approval. Now Daoud is unsure of how to proceed. If
Susan's parents had been in the same city, he would have
sent musicians to her family and gone with his parents, all
arms laden with gifts, to make a formal proposal. He
considers arranging musicians and gifts through a cousin
in the States, but he doesn't want to burden his cousin with
such a complicated mission, and besides, there would be
so many ways in which the plan could go wrong.

Even though Daoud is a progressive-thinking
philosopher, the importance of this event transforms him.
His love for Susan has confused Daoud, who once felt
himself too strong for such reckless emotion. He is
surprised to realise how her glance towards him can warm
him and how a glance away can upset him. He longs for
her, sometimes in her very presence. Suddenly the old
traditions are worth following, even if Susan's parents are
far away.

He creates a video for Susan's family, showing them
scenes around Kelaat M'Gouna – the school where he first
saw Susan, the rose fields where she works with the
families. Then, in Fez, he films his family home,
introducing them to his parents and sister. With his closest
friends as camera crew, Daoud takes the viewers on a tour
of his neighbourhood and city. Luck brings a group of

musicians singing a marriage proposal outside a grand home, and Daoud's friend, with a mischievous grin, films some close shots of the drums and horns and singers.

They film a wandering herd mixed of sheep and camels outside of the city; they pass through the most narrow and crowded passages of the market, holding the camera tightly so as not to have it jostled. The film captures people as they flatten themselves against the old and venerable walls of the market to allow for the passage of carts laden with grains and other plants. They film tannery workers as they dye and pound large canvases of leather, and the rhythmic, ringing sounds of the metal workers.

They even go into a dress shop, where a tailor is persuaded to hold up several dresses to show Susan's family the many different dresses Susan might wear during a wedding ceremony that would require her to wear at least seven different changes of costume, jewellery, and make-up.

Daoud grew up near the oldest university in the world, Al Karaouine, and as a child, he often glimpsed visions of the scholars at work there within its intricately designed walls, its beautifully tiled fountains, and its luxurious carpets. These visions of scholars at their work initiated Daoud's desire to study, and although he never studied in Fez, but rather in Rabat, he always stops when he reaches the doors of Al Karaouine, just to spend a few minutes watching the scholars for inspiration.

He regrets that he cannot share this vision on Susan's video, for her family to see, but he knows it would be inappropriate to film the scholars or the beauty of the university for his personal gain. This is a sacred place, belonging to God alone. Daoud vows to walk along this path one day with Susan and her parents, and he smiles at the idea of watching their faces when they first view a glimpse through the open doors.

Towards the end of the video, Umar and Khadija give eloquent, warm, welcoming speeches in Arabic that Daoud translates. His sister tries, but she is so shy in front of the camera that Daoud can hardly recognise her. Then Daoud is alone, speaking frankly in English to tell Susan's family about his feelings and his commitment to them all. He tells them of his love for their daughter, how he never planned to marry outside of his family's acquaintances, and how she has captured his attention and admiration.

Once they finish the video, Daoud makes three copies to ensure their safe arrival. He asks one cousin who is travelling to the States to mail a copy from there, but Daoud doesn't trust this method of delivery, and therefore arranges for a second copy to be mailed from France. The third copy Daoud mails himself, from Fez.

His hope is that at least one of the videos will arrive safely with Susan's family, but in fact, all three arrive, each a week apart. Susan's parents watch the first video as soon as it arrives from France. They are touched by Daoud's novel proposal, and they become very emotional listening to his final speech. When the second package arrives from Morocco, they watch it from start to finish, assuming there will be some difference. When the third package arrives from New York, they watch it in fast-forward, just in case.

The first time that Susan hears about this video or the proposal is when her parents call to ask her what she thinks about it. In fact, Susan does not see this video at all until several years later, when she and Daoud finally visit her parents' home. Once she has a copy in her possession, however, Susan watches it often, each time breaking down in tears when Daoud tells her parents how he loves her.

It is, perhaps, the existence of this video that has prevented many marital spats from ever beginning. Susan needs only remember the video and it is impossible for her to be angry with Daoud for any small thing.

Daoud's parents, Khadija and Umar, love weddings. Every detail of a wedding brings a memory and a joy. They attend every wedding they are invited to, even if they have to travel far. Their love for weddings keeps them particularly busy in the month before Ramadan, when many weddings occur. In this month of weddings, they might attend two or three in a single day.

Why do they love weddings so much? Partly because they love their own marriage. They enjoy one another's company, always have. In fact, they have never known life without the other. As children, their parents lived close, and the families often spent time together. Their relationship was nurtured by their parents, but there was never a need to force the idea of marriage upon either of them. Their parents were grateful for the ease with which it seemed to evolve, from childhood friendship to marriage.

For Khadija and Umar, Amal's decision not to marry is their personal failure and disappointment. Because their life together is rich and fulfilling, they wish the same for their children. And when Daoud brings Susan home, they feel both happy and yet sceptical.

"This girl might take him away from us," Khadija worries.

"She might. We can't know. God will decide it," is her husband's typical response.

"They could make beautiful children."

"Yes, they certainly could."

"But what good is it to have beautiful grandchildren if we can never see them?"

"You met Susan today; already you have grandchildren!" Umar laughs. "I like her. She has a good heart."

"Amal may never marry."

"Don't concern yourself with that, Khadija. Amal says the love in this house is enough for her."

"But it's not. She should have more. She should have what we have."

"She could also have less. Many women her age have troubled marriages. Let's be thankful."

Umar is always quiet at the close of the day. He has prayed each of his prayers, and he is content to lie close to his wife and listen to her breathing. Before he sleeps, though, he always reaches for her with a new surprise. Each night he concentrates his attention on some neglected part of her body, and with each new day, Khadija wonders what her husband will do to please her in the coming night. This day he has been thinking of her knees. The first time he saw her knees was after their wedding when he tickled them, and she giggled. Tonight it is the same.

Their own wedding lasted a week. The guests came from all over the country and from France, and the ceremonial traditions were followed in great detail. Umar looked forward with anxiety and excitement to finally be alone with her, but first he had to go through the many dances, songs, recitations, meals, changes of clothing, processions, and prayers.

When Daoud's wedding is just a week away, guests begin arriving from many places. Umar is busily preparing rooms to accommodate them with local friends and family. A friend owns a small hotel, and he is disposed to assist in an overflow emergency. Umar is particularly concerned about the guests of honour: Susan's parents, sister, and grandmother, who will make their first trip to Morocco from the United States. He wants to assure a good visit for everyone.

Khadija is planning also. She, too, wants Susan's family to enjoy every minute of their wedding. Khadija and Amal have collected all of the dresses that Susan needs for the many processions, showing each of the regional dresses of Morocco. They have added a white dress, Susan's final dress, to represent the United States. Khadija wonders how Susan and her family will react to all of the Moroccan customs, but Amal reassures her.

"We just have to tell them exactly what to expect, Mama. They will all have a good time here. I can't wait to see Susan carried high in the Amarya. I hope she isn't scared."

"Let's assure that your wild cousins are not the ones to carry her. Remember last year? I thought they would drop that poor country girl who married Yusuf."

In the midst of this planning, Daoud seeks a few minutes alone with his mother: "Mama, I need to talk with you."

"What is it, Daoud?" His mother's eyes are sparkling, as they always do on special occasions.

Daoud needs to address a rather delicate matter – the inspection of the bridal sheets on the morning after the wedding. This is one aspect of the ceremony that Daoud would like to avoid, lest he disappoint his family. His mother's eyes stop sparkling and darken over when she sees her son's anxious face.

"What is it, my dear son?" she asks, her hand moving instinctively to his cheeks and brow.

"You know, Susan and I, I mean, well, she isn't going to pass that inspection, Mother."

Khadija laughs at Daoud in his discomfort, not a bit surprised: "You and Susan are adults, Daoud, well beyond the age of my own wedding. Virgin brides are to be expected when they are fourteen or fifteen years old, but Susan is twenty-four!" Now Daoud laughs with his mother in relief. Khadija shakes her head, laughing, thinking of how son must have suffered as he prepared for this conversation.

"My son, don't even think of it. I am two steps ahead of you." She goes to the cupboard for the vial of red liquid she will spill on the sheets before removing them from the bed, singing with joy and lifting them on high above the heads of her guests. Umar's sister has helped to prepare the vial so that the colour and consistency is perfect.

(Mis) communication

Every evening in the village square of Taroudant, in the markets at Marrakesh, and in countless other places around the country, crowds gather in concentric layers around a storyteller, whose wild, outrageous stories have been the object of anticipation throughout the day. Hundreds of men circle around – not only to listen, but to interject and influence the outcome of the day's story. Across the street sit men in cafés, all facing the same direction to watch the dramas of passers-by and to gossip over the day's events. So many stories going on around me, and I strain to know the words.

Sometimes I yearn to speak Arabic; sometimes I despair of ever learning. When I feel my deficiency most acutely is in Taroudant, where talk goes on at a constant pulse, where the family of my beloved engages in rich and vibrant dialogues. Oh how I romanticise these! They could be asking one another to pass the salt, while I imagine the solutions to intricate and complicated puzzles being offered to my oblivious ear.

In my daily struggle to learn Moroccan Arabic are resonant tones and timbres in full range, a vast compendium of words that transforms fluidly to suit a context, and sounds that are impossible for me to form: my throat never having been called upon to create such sounds before. Being a language learner is infantilising. I struggle valiantly for status as an adult, while loved ones look with sympathy and speak in the simplest of terms in their attempts to reach me. Were I you, my beloved, a brilliant and ready linguist, I would have become a fluent speaker quite easily. But not being you, I struggle along wretchedly, my own very limited self.

Once as we approach a low-hanging bridge over our walking path, a man on a bicycle rides towards us, shouting in shrill and impassioned tones. Had I been alone, I would have feared him, but my beloved explains that he is simply cautioning us so that we don't bump our heads on the ceiling. I think then of how easily we misinterpret one another, even in the same language. Here we have been met by kindness, and yet my response is more apprehensive than grateful.

I know how Susan feels when she is introduced to Moroccan Arabic. As new learners, we rely heavily on context and gestures in our first attempts to communicate, and our patient first listeners help us by tuning in carefully and correcting us gently. Like Susan, I have moments of frustration and of celebration, as I am increasingly able to participate in the conversations around me.

Moroccan Arabic becomes a puzzle to solve, a fascination. To learn Moroccan Arabic, for someone who was raised in a Latinate or Germanic language, is to throw out all the old rules: conjugations take place in any part of a word, plurals can be indicated by a change in the middle, marking vowels is optional, and rules of capitalisation are replaced by variations in initial, medial, and final characters. As a left-handed person, I appreciate a language that moves right to left: my hand no longer passes across fresh ink, and my writing is no longer marred by smudges across the page.

As I become aware of the subtleties of Moroccan Arabic, I find my thoughts shaping to the expressions of my new language. Language is more than just a system of words and grammar; the subtleties of a language can also shape one's thoughts and perspective. As I become more attuned to humour, sarcasm, and innuendo, I wake sometimes to realise that my parents have been speaking Moroccan Arabic in my dreams or I have been bargaining with Moroccan merchants in English.

It is partly due to my embrace of Moroccan Arabic that I begin to feel drawn to the Qur'an, curious about the faith of the prophets and the traditions that started with Abraham, Moses, Jesus, Mohammed, and their many generations of believers. In Morocco, there is a specific context for Islam, its text and believers, and because the community is so kind and gentle, I begin to imagine a place for myself among them. When this happens, it is as if light shines from me and reaches towards me, and I believe this light could protect me from mishaps and dangers.

At first I felt excluded because I couldn't walk into a mosque. I was not a Muslim, and I was not allowed. What was the feeling, exactly? Disappointment? Irritation? Rejection? The building is not only a marvel of architecture, but also a privilege. I would sometimes glimpse through an open door, feel drawn towards the open spaces inside. What I understand now is that it isn't a question of exclusion but rather of humility. Coming to God for prayer requires more than desire: it requires physical and mental preparation, a thorough washing of the body in accordance with the Qur'an, and the proper covering for both men and women.

There are overwhelmingly pleasant smells in Morocco: warm bread in a bakery, cinnamon and saffron in the warmth of a stew, the fragrance of rose oils and argan as women walk home from hammam.

But wherever there are fruit trees and hot temperatures, there is the unpleasant smell of fermenting and rotting fruit. In Morocco, I am often inundated with various smells, bringing memories of other tropical climes.

The smell on my mind at the moment is of rotten fruit and ammonia, and particularly strong in the second floor of the building where we go twice in one week for the notary. We pass a first floor with large full sacks of flour, guarded by three men in military uniform (is it really flour then? Or something else? I wonder); we climb a flight of stairs.

The smell on this day is particularly pungent, reaching past my nose and into my sinuses. I feel this smell in my ears and my throat. I follow my beloved and the stranger who has come to buy our car, slowly because my sandals catch on the irregular stairs. I arrive at the top of the flight alone, no longer seeing my beloved or our companion. I wonder now whether to enter the office door ahead or to climb another tall flight. Seeing my hesitation and somehow knowing what I should do, a man near me kindly gestures towards the office door.

Often in Morocco, especially in government work, there are several employees assigned to tasks that could probably be given to one. This may seem an inefficient system, but it means that people remain employed. The king, as the nation's most active employer, seems to prefer to pay people for working rather than developing a system of welfare that could encourage people to stay home and collect benefits.

In the regional notary office, there are three workers. The first stamps the paper with black ink and with red and green stamps like the Moroccan flag. The second checks our identifications, registers our names, and takes our thumbprints. The third sits alone at an empty desk with no apparent duties. Perhaps he is keeping us safe or waiting for his turn at a desk. The first man wears a soccer jersey, and I wonder if he remembers us from our last visit. We were here one week ago, when this man took ten dirhams from my beloved without offering the proper change of four dirhams. And this happened during

Ramadan, when such transgressions are especially grievous. This time, my beloved offers only two dirhams instead of six, just to see what will happen: the man's face seems to register two thoughts in quick order: first a dispute, then a recognition. He says nothing to protest.

This scene reminds me of a bank in Azrou, where three people are always there, and no matter when we visit, they always sit in the same formation: the young woman in the middle, behind an empty desk with seemingly nothing to do, and the men on either side with various papers and duties of collecting, counting, and reporting on financial transactions.

The smell in this bank is clear and crisp, and the air is pleasantly cool. In the States it is always a shock to the body to enter an air-conditioned building on a hot day. Americans have the habit of extreme temperatures: on cold days the buildings are warmed excessively, while on hot days they are cooled too much. Americans must wear various layers of clothing to respond to these wild fluctuations of temperature from inside to out. In Morocco, the air conditioning is only used sparingly, to take the edge off a hot day; on cold days the heating is subtle, a gentle warming of a room. I often wonder why we Americans seem to revel in excess: not only unnecessary, but inconvenient.

Elizabeth in Tangier

Elizabeth returns to the hotel, tired but exhilarated. In the lobby, she sees Valene, the woman staying in the next room, for whom Elizabeth carried a suitcase on the day before. "Let me treat you for dinner," says Valene. "I don't mind travelling alone, but when it comes to dinner, I simply must have company." Elizabeth hasn't spoken to anyone since Mahmoud left her at the train station, and she has a lot to say. Valene orders an expensive bottle of wine. "My treat, I said," as she sees Elizabeth's nervous glance at the prices, "and order anything you wish."

Soon they are happily chatting about their common interests in art and French literature, and only later does Elizabeth tell Valene about Mahmoud.

"Where is he now?" Valene asks.

"His uncle is sick," replies Elizabeth, "so he went to visit."

"But where?"

"Tétouan, I think," says Elizabeth, "or was it Chefchaouen? I can't remember." The truth is, he said Tétouan on one occasion and then Chefchaouen on another. Elizabeth doesn't say this out loud, though, because she thinks it sounds suspicious.

It is true that Valene is suspicious. Why Chefchaouen, for example? She knows that some young people use Chefchaouen as a code word for a place to find illicit drugs. Was he being facetious? But beyond that – why would Mahmoud have an uncle in the north when the rest of his family lives in the south? It's not impossible, certainly, but it doesn't seem likely, and in any case, it's curious to Valene that he would visit his uncle alone. Why wouldn't his parents or his sisters join him? And why wouldn't he take Elizabeth? But Valene, in spite of her scepticism, says nothing about it to Elizabeth. Remember that Sophie, Sanaa, and Susan confronted Elizabeth, more or less directly? Valene has more subtle tactics. Instead, she invites Elizabeth to Tangier, promising fabulous art galleries, a famous bookstore, and a viewing of Valene's own private art collection, including one canvas in particular that Elizabeth will recognise from her art history textbooks. The next morning, Valene's driver appears in a long sedan, and they drive away to Tangier. In the car is an architectural magazine that has recently featured Valene's current home with "before" and "after" photographs that highlight elegant renovations. Valene will soon sell the place for a glorious profit and begin again with another.

When they arrive at this lovely home, Valene instructs the cooking staff — two sisters whose pastillas and tagines are famously delicious. A continual stream of visitors passes through the courtyard. There is a ragged man bringing pills that Valene claims are painkillers for her back. There is a professor from the University of Granada in Melilla who has travelled quite a distance, including an international border, just to bring a book for Valene and who seems disappointed to see Elizabeth there. There is a man who offers to trim the trees in her courtyard. There is a gallery owner who wants her advice. A young artist comes humbly by, asking Valene for a donation for paints and canvases. She gives him some money, a loaf of bread, and some encouraging words.

Valene is absolutely the real thing, and if you go to Tangier today you won't miss her. Her upturned nose, eyes glancing down to survey her reign, the forward thrust of her ample chest, her sparkling, strappy heels: Valene is all show and glow, at the top of her game among the powerful elite. She could call almost any CEO or politician in the country to enforce her will, and she often does, as many men either owe her a favour or hope to earn her favour. She has seen them in every kind of position – from their most powerful moments to their most vulnerable and naked. She fascinates and terrifies at once.

Valene made a fortune in her younger days, and she continues to develop her wealth while defying her ageing body. No matter that her back aches to a crippling degree and her grey roots are a constant battle. Valene forges ahead boldly, walking along cobblestone streets in high heels without even stumbling. Once Valene spent too much time in the Moroccan countryside and had to travel eight hours to Rabat to restore her hair's blond glory. Blond hair, for Valene, is essential to her gig.

Don't be mistaken: Valene may seem a feminine beauty, a purring kitten, but never associate her femininity with weakness, as too many unfortunate men have done. Valene wields real power. Men all over Tangier, and in many other corners of the world, tremble (some with pleasure, some with utter fear) at the sound of her name, and each of them, motivated by pleasure or fear, would go to great lengths to serve her or to satisfy her demands.

Like her father before her, Valene lives by subjugating others. But Valene's subjects are neither impoverished nor defenceless, and so we might wonder how she continues to thrive, with so many wishing her dead, but the truth is that Valene lives, like her father did, at her own peril. Her risks are calibrated – not only for survival but also for maximum gain.

Valene says nothing to Elizabeth about her own failed marriage to a Saudi prince, but this is just Valene's way. She keeps a few secrets to herself, and especially this one. Instead, she tells Elizabeth about her childhood in Zimbabwe, when the country was still Rhodesia, and the horses she loved and left behind.

Valene's British parents were ranchers in southern Africa. When Valene was born, the indigenous black citizens were fighting for their independence from white minority rule. On Valene's fifth birthday, Zimbabwe declared its independence, but unilaterally. It took fifteen years for this independence to be recognised abroad.

Perhaps it was fifteen years before all the white rulers and ranchers lost their grip on power, but for Valene's family, it happened much faster. It took only five years for her family to disintegrate: for her father to be killed, for her brother to wander away, for her mother to become a living ghost.

Valene's father died because his living depended on his ability to colonise majority populations. Because he was arrogant, he believed in his own strength. Because of his physical strength, he believed that he held the destiny of his family in his own hands. Because he was foolish, he didn't realise that their precarious method of living could only function as long as there were structures in place to support it. As the structures of white rule in Zimbabwe began to collapse and crumble, the ruling minority was easily defeated. Valene's father became an early casualty – not because he was weak, but because he was cruel.

Valene's older brother, distraught by his father's death and the inevitable loss of his fortune, left his mother and younger sister one day and wandered off, never to be heard from again. Valene was left then, alone with the shadow of a mother. Unable to leave their home, they depended on a few of their past employees who took pity on them, bringing them food and water in the night.

Once, they had considered themselves benevolent, genteel ranchers on a lucrative plot of land; now they were asked to see themselves in a new way: as greedy and ruthless colonisers, convicted by popular opinion. Her mother couldn't do it, and retreated to her bedroom instead, where she would read her Bible and wait, expecting soon to pass through an earthly fire into paradise.

But young Valene, to her credit, looked at herself in the mirror that the indigenous people were holding, and she realised the truth about her family. They didn't belong in Zimbabwe, and they were doing damage. She promised herself then that she would become a good person. She did not feel like a good person, but she would learn. If she became wealthy, she would be unselfish. She was determined to live in a new way.

For many months, Valene would lean against her mother's bedroom doorframe, watching the woman, asking questions of her, making requests. Valene wanted to use words to keep her mother alive, but it was hopeless. Over time, she stopped answering Valene, even stopped opening her eyes except for a few moments each day.

When she wasn't watching her mother, Valene watched through the slats of the windows as the land was divided into small plots, populated by the people she had always known. The redistribution of land was definitive but unofficial for the fifteen years between Zimbabwe's declaration of independence and its international recognition as an independent nation. By the time Zimbabweans gained their national charter and their titles to the land, Valene would be far away and forgotten.

One day a neighbour comes, offering to take Valene and her mother with his family. They have decided to go home, to England. Valene's mother can barely shake her head in refusal, but Valene understands. Her mother has always been stubborn about England because of the insults she endured from her father at their final farewell. She swore then to never return.

But Valene wants to go. She wants to be released from the prison that her home has become. The neighbour will hire a former servant to care for his own mother who has also insisted on staying behind, and he will pay a bit more so that Valene's mother can also receive care. They will live together in the same house, and they will be left in peace as the small farms are established around them. There will be food and shelter. They will be comfortable, even if they are lonely and unhappy. Sometimes there is nothing else to be done.

Valene expects to be treated poorly, like an orphan in a sad British novel, but she is pleasantly surprised when her grandparents open their arms in welcome to her. Under her grandfather's direction, Valene is tutored in the various disciplines expected of an aristocratic child, and she excels in French and fencing. She rides like a princess, caring lovingly for the horses. Valene impresses her grandfather, who expected this African grandchild to arrive with a wild and rough demeanour. Instead, Valene charms the old man, who declares her more elegant and refined than his English-born grandchildren. To the dismay of other relatives, Valene becomes his favoured one, and he begins to groom her as a business partner.

But this partnership is not to be – for two reasons. The first is that her grandfather dies before he can settle his accounts and assure Valene's place. The surviving relatives provide Valene with a reasonable share of the inheritance, and Valene, with her characteristic dignity, accepts their offering and turns her back on England.

The second reason is that Valene is indeed an African child in many ways. Raised without limits of distance or time, she woke every day to the sun and its winds. The horses of Zimbabwe are taller and stronger, and Valene prefers to ride at a full gallop across unending plains.

She seems quite young when, at eighteen, she marries a Saudi man with access to a small fortune. Luckily for him he trusts her business acumen, and she guides him in multiplying his wealth many times over. But marriage doesn't suit Valene. She finds it tiresome. They remain business partners to this day, however, and they continue to reap the rewards of their partnership.

So this is Valene, Elizabeth's only friend in Morocco. Elizabeth watches Valene as she receives her many guests, pours their tea, provides whatever advice or assistance she can. Elizabeth is amazed by her friend, and inspired. And Elizabeth is sketching. She is always sketching now. Because Valene is so popular, Elizabeth can sit near her, in the courtyard or the local café, quietly sketching while Valene holds conversations with her various acquaintances. In some ways it is like being at home with her mother, Elizabeth thinks. When she realises that Valene is like her mother, she wonders: why do I like this woman so much? And why am I so impatient with my mother?

Valene admires Elizabeth's sketches and encourages her to work with them. There's a studio upstairs, a bright and welcoming studio, and Valene wants Elizabeth to use it. There are canvases and paints, and Elizabeth can stay as long as she wishes. She could paint and turn those sketches into marketable works of art. Valene is so kind and thoughtful that Elizabeth is tempted to stay for many months, painting and selling her work as she has always wanted to do.

But Elizabeth has one last unfortunate stumbling block, and it will be a long and disastrous stumble. The problem is that Elizabeth is feeling anxious. Her voyage to

Tangier, hasty and reckless, had been a desperate attempt to forget Mahmoud, but it hasn't worked. When Mahmoud first texts her, Elizabeth responds with a cool and coy detachment, but as each day closes upon itself, Elizabeth turns from nonchalant to hysterical, disconsolate: she misses Mahmoud terribly.

Valene has enjoyed Elizabeth's company and would continue to do so, but she is not one to insist. After she calls her driver to take Elizabeth to the train, she repeats her invitation – "You may return at any time, Elizabeth. My door is always open to you, and it would be a pleasure to see those sketches come to life."

A family

February, 2010

"Forgive her, Susan," he begged of me then, "and forgive me, even more. This will never come between us again."

Daoud begged me to forgive him, and I did. I wasn't ready, but I did. His mother's suggestion that he marry a second wife, well, it cut into me and left a lasting scar. For a long time, I could only see Khadija as an enemy, and it took a long time for me to change that.

I realise now that she was trying to help us. She thought my work was too demanding. But really, it was her insistence on children and housework and cleaning, and I suppose I still resent it some. I don't have the same vision that she has. I don't believe that we are obligated to have children or keep house in a certain way. And truly, her insistence on our gender roles has been a hindrance in my marriage. I need Daoud to be an equal

partner at home, to do his share of
housework and cooking. He knows this on
a certain level, but there's also a way
in which he sides with his mother.

Daoud and I have many secrets like this
between us. Most of them are happy ones.
We enjoy living in a private world that
we share with no one else. Our secrets
aren't particularly earth-shaking –
just small things that amuse us and
memories that no one else could have.
Once the children came along, we let
them in on some of these secrets, but
not all. It is because of our privacy
that Salma asks so many questions. As
our oldest child and only daughter, she
seems determined to crack every code
and delve into the world of her parents.
I'll never tell my children about
Khadijah's proposal, but I'll never
forget it, either. I've forgiven her,
and I have the children because of her
insistence. I wasn't grateful for her
intervention, but I'm grateful about
the children. I wouldn't have known
this kind of love without her.

One memory Daoud and Susan share is of their special day
at Lexis and the plans they made together on that day.
Daoud, after gaining permission from his parents and from
Susan's parents to marry her, invites Susan to the ancient
grounds of Lexis. He wants to wander with her among the
ancient buildings. He wants her to feel this very breeze
and to see these ancient trees. Daoud has chosen this place
to talk with Susan about the marriage they want to build

together, and he wants to have this conversation at Lexis – a place of secure and sturdy buildings that have withstood the winds and rains of millennia.

Susan and Daoud walk together among the trees and grasses, the stone arches of the buildings, still holding up the weight of history. The place still speaks of a vibrant community of performers, protectors, and providers.

Many people admire the marriage of Daoud and Susan, their continuing affection for one another, the unique partnership they have built. One of their secrets is that they worked things out together on one miraculous day on the hills of Lexis.

Their daughter Salma often asks them about their wedding. These are questions about her origin: she wants to know where she comes from. "Tell me about the wedding," she might say. "Was it cold or sunny on those days?" Her questions change slightly each time, but she knows exactly what she is doing. After these many years, Salma could tell the story of her parents' wedding better than anyone, yet she never does. She likes it to be told to her.

Her parents have told the story to Salma many times: with her, they cannot change a single detail, as she has formed an inviolable narrative in her mind. When she was younger, she would ask for the story in its entirety, but lately she has refined her methods. Cleverly, she asks for bits and pieces, checking for gaps or discrepancies, asking each parent separately about the details of their four-day wedding. She isolates each parent because she is checking the facts, and if any detail seems ruffled or misplaced, she brings a challenge forth, insisting on absolute precision.

Often children are curious about the lives of their parents. What were they like before becoming parents?

How did parenting change them? Some children like to know their impact.

Salma, Adel, and Isaac are different from other children. They speak Moroccan Arabic in private, at home, and they speak English in public. Hardly anyone knows this.

When they travel, they go to Morocco, unlike their friends who go to amusement parks and campgrounds. Sometimes they are jealous of their friends, but more often, their friends are the ones to be jealous.

When bombs destroyed the World Trade Center, just a few miles away in New York, the children could smell the acrid odours on the wind. They watched the television as the official story unfolded about Muslim terrorists and plots against their country. Unlike their neighbours and the families at school, Susan and Daoud reacted with suspicion: they questioned the official story as it unfolded on television, and this was yet another way in which their family feels set apart from the others.

Sometimes Adel feels proud of his family for being different, but when it comes to being an Arab child in upstate New York and feeling his Muslim community accused, however falsely, of crimes against humanity, he definitely does not want his family to be quite so strange and unusual.

Zahra's Ifrane

The best of Morocco is always compared to Europe in such an exasperating way, as if Morocco were incapable of producing or sustaining anything good of its own. The lovely village of Ifrane, high in the mountains with its waterfalls and lush parks, is so clean and sweet as to be declared a Swiss village rather than an elegant Moroccan town. Likewise, my beloved is so good and sweet that people call him Americanised rather than recognise all the Moroccan kindness that he carries abroad.

Ifrane is so lovely that Morocco must fully claim it as its own, yet I often hear Moroccans describe it as a European beauty. A royal palace and its grounds are located in Ifrane, and the royal university also. The rest is a town of winding wooded pathways, village squares with lighted fountains, and large, often-vacant houses topped with large nests for enormous families of cranes. Ifrane may resemble an Alpine village by its geography, climate, and architecture, but the place belongs fully to Morocco, and its sweetness is absolutely Moroccan.

Sometimes in the States, I try to describe the beauty of Ifrane to others. I labour over the details, trying to share with my listener how very special it is. My listener, perhaps bored, perhaps incredulous, nods along until finally I find myself falling into the same heretical trap that I criticise, and I say that Ifrane is often compared to a Swiss Alpine village. And here my listener lights up, registering surprise and interest: "Oh really? I hear

Switzerland is beautiful! Is Ifrane really so lovely? Who would have guessed it?" Indeed. I achieve this response at the cost of my integrity, and there it is, another compromise.

Many Moroccans spend their summer vacations in Ifrane to walk along its pathways and breathe its light, crisp air. At the centre of the university campus is a large and ornate mosque. The campus has one of the most beautiful and well-appointed libraries in the nation, various large classroom and office buildings, a full-scale dining operation with restaurants of various styles, an Olympic-sized pool, athletic training facilities, ample office space, residences for students and personnel, and all the latest technology.

Mahmoud walks alone on the vast lawn, carrying his beloved book – Bhabha, of course, and nothing less. He greets a man in passing, and they talk for a few minutes together. When the man asks about the book, Mahmoud takes a breath, preparing to launch into his well-rehearsed lecture regarding his disagreements with some of the finer points, but the man interrupts: "Are you planning to read during the ceremony?" He teases, "maybe you should spend more time in the library if you aren't yet prepared to graduate." Laughing at his own joke, the man wanders off towards the gym, and Mahmoud waits a few minutes before following him inside to the ceremony.

Decorated for graduation in red and gold fabrics, the gym shows off its triangular architecture. Sunlight filters gently through large windows. The crowd murmurs quietly until the Andalusian music begins: then silence. The graduates enter handsomely in pairs, dressed in black suits with white shirts and blouses. Some women wear skirts, some pants. Some women wear veils, but most do not.

When the university president addresses the graduates, he reminds them to remain avid readers and writers, reflecting on current developments in their fields, solving complex problems, and adapting to changing conditions. His speech addresses the highest ideals of a liberal arts education, "Social scientists examine the structures of communities and how we might envision our future; scientists and mathematicians observe phenomena, express hypotheses, and evaluate degrees of certainty." He speaks directly to the graduates, his eyes fixed upon them: "You have met physical challenges in your athletic courses and competitions. You have analysed the aesthetic pleasure of artistic creations. You have come to understand the perspectives of others and see the role of history in our current global context. Whether discovering the beauty of poetry, peering into a cylinder radio telescope, or unravelling the mysteries of human history, you are learning more than facts: you are learning to think independently and make sound judgements. You are expanding your horizons, discovering new perspectives, and acquiring tools to defend your point of view."

We watch Mahmoud from a few rows behind him, and it seems as if he might swoon. Overcome by the emotion of the speech, he closes his eyes, nodding his head fervently in agreement. Then he springs to life, inspired. He takes a small notebook and pen from his pocket and writes furiously, trying to capture the president's words.

After the ceremony, we see the American ambassador when he is already moving towards us, arms outstretched for one of his famous ambassador bear hugs. In a country where I am rarely hugged by any man other than my beloved, this vision of a hug moving towards me creates a mixed emotion of apprehension and delight. Fully aware of the thousand eyes upon me, the crowd of curious onlookers, and my beloved's amusement, the ambassador's hug is that of a long-lost uncle: warm, sustained, and kind.

The ambassador has rare qualities for a diplomat: he is sincere, plain-spoken, and unpretentious. Later his wife and I walk along a grassy expanse, away from the ceremony. The mother of a graduate runs to catch up with us because she has something she wants to say. She wants to tell the ambassador's wife how admirable she is, how very different she is from the Moroccan wives of dignitaries. She is anxious to say that the ambassador's wife is nothing like those Moroccan elite, who dress extravagantly and wear their hair in fancy styles. "You are nothing like them," the woman says.

I believe she means to compliment, but the inelegance of her words rests heavily on our threesome. No one knows quite what to say, as the ambassador's wife pats her hair uncertainly and pulls down on her simple blouse. I feel with her a collective Midwestern-ness, a certain kinship of the plainly dressed. I cringe through the awkward moment and hope it soon passes. And yes, the woman moves away, perhaps belatedly embarrassed if she has realised her error, perhaps oblivious, and my companion and I are alone again in the crowd, drifting uncertainly, and far from home.

Royal family

It may be true that no one on earth enjoys a jet ski as much as the young king, Mohammed VI. No one else on earth has so much at stake on the ride, nor such a desperate need for the liberating properties that the vehicle affords him. Only on the jet ski is the king truly free. The noise of the water and machine assure that no voice can intrude on his thoughts, and though his guards surround him on similar vehicles, and his boats and helicopters circle close, they cannot disturb him. And this, for the king, is a rare moment of freedom.

Mohammed VI, who became king after his father's death in 1999, is a bit more relaxed than his father, whose rule was strict and brooked no dissent. The son is considered a benevolent man. Each year, on a hot day in July, crowds of officials, soldiers, and citizens stand in the plazas for hours to offer their best wishes to their king on the anniversary of his ascension to the throne. On this day, the king releases hundreds of prisoners and visits people who are sick and impoverished. On the way to his ceremony, he stops at random government offices to fire corrupt officials.

Each year, the celebration takes place in a different city, renewed and enlivened by the honour of being the chosen place. Being the chosen place for the ceremonies also means a chance at urban renewal – a budget for beautification and repairs. Streets are paved with fresh tar, and roundabouts are installed at the busiest four-way intersections. Crumbling walls and pillars are patched and painted. One summer day we watch as hundreds of trucks and military vehicles arrive for the ceremony in Tétouan. Regiments gather from each region of the country to salute their king. The top officials stand for hours in formation. The young prince stands straight and tall beside his father: a dignified child, ready to carry the burden of leadership on his little shoulders. The king's brother stands on the other side, always at the ready.

Then a year later, the Arab world erupts with revolutions. Not only the Arab world, but it seems the entire world is in motion: Angola, Azerbaijan, China, Georgia, Italy, Malaysia, Romania, Uganda, even the state of Wisconsin, whose union leaders receive a video message of support from Tahrir Square in Cairo.

The response of each leader is unpredictable. The president of Tunisia sends his wife out of the country with a stack of gold bricks, and he follows soon after, resting safely abroad until the Tunisian courts convict him in absentia.

Then Egyptians fight valiantly, many to the death, through weeks of violence. President Mubarak seems intractable until the end, when he retires abruptly. Soon his sons are in jail, and Mubarak takes refuge in the hospital after staging multiple heart attacks.

Libya's Qaddafi promises to go on a door-to-door killing spree in a speech that is rapidly converted into an irreverent song played in nightclubs. He is killed in a humiliating final scene in Sirte, which is described in the press like the end of Richard III: Qaddafi running from a car to a house, then crawling on his belly through the desert and into a drainage pipe, where he is shot, first by enemies and then by friends who hope to save him from further humiliation. But he emerges with the gunshot wounds into the desert where he is beaten, poked with sticks, and finally shot again, this time mortally.

The presidents of Yemen, Syria, and Egypt are accused of using nerve gas and other violent methods against their protesters, but the Arab kings are more subtle in responding to public demands. The king of Saudi Arabia, from a hospital bed in the United States, offers large stipends to his population, hoping for a peaceful return home. He even declares that women will soon vote and hold public office, but his population still simmers in unrest, and the women of Saudi Arabia take to the wheels of their family cars, asking the American Secretary of State to support them in lifting the ban against female drivers.

Syrians attempt an underground protest, hoping for support from outside, but they miscalculate the promises of the Americans. There is no help for them against their cruel and crushing president. For them it is death and destruction – the people and their ancient cities, and the lucky ones find some shelter in Turkey and elsewhere.

Meanwhile, protesters rage in Algeria, Bahrain, Djibouti, Iran, Iraq, Jordan, Kuwait, Lebanon, Mauritania, Oman, Palestine, and Sudan. Some leaders make concessions, while others make none. In some nations the concessions of the leaders are enough; in others, there is no way to quell the protests.

In Morocco, certainly the king notices what is happening in the world, and he sees at least one encampment of displaced workers outside the palace, their numbers growing each day.

The people of the Rif, the northern Moroccans, are well known for their strength in battle. Many times has the Rif guarded the rest of the nation from invaders from the north or the east. The king often spends his vacations in the Rif area, maintaining a relationship of fidelity. He invests heavily in the north, providing jobs and services.

But in spite of his close attention, the Rif is the first region where violence occurs during the protests of 2011. While the protesters in Rabat, Casablanca, and other points to the south hold peaceful marches, the Rif suffers fires and looting. All over the country, Moroccans begin to protest in large numbers, mostly in peace, and the king urges his military to exercise restraint.

World leaders commend Mohammed VI and his military for their peaceful methods, but then there is violence in Kenifra, and the police forget their instructions to be peaceful. Now the king must respond: reform the constitution or watch the country spiral into violence.

Unlike his counterparts in other nations, the king proposes a long list of changes to the national constitution. On a Wednesday in March, he announces these historic reforms on television to a rapt nation. His speech is humble: he will be prayerful and look to guidance from God in his goal of creating a better place for his people. He suggests the following: the declaration of Tamazight as an official language, the need for rule of law and freedoms, an independent judiciary and separation of powers, free elections and regional representation, and increased accountability in all government institutions. He plans to elevate the position of prime minister, offering independent, executive powers, in some areas surpassing the powers of the king.

The Moroccan people respond, some with scepticism and some with enthusiasm. They rush out into the streets, some to celebrate their king and others to pressure him. Morocco has the opportunity to become an international leader in reform, and the people embrace this concept. For some, embracing the concept means continuing to march, and these marchers organise well, maintaining a respectful dissent. Watching reports on our laptops from the safety of our American apartment, my beloved and I cheer them all: protesters and leaders alike. We also prepare for our summer travels that will begin in Rabat.

Why Rabat? Not for any academic purpose but for the music festival, Mawazine, that we enjoy. One year we stood near the stage as Sting sang down to us for hours. Then the protests begin to centre around this concert, calling for its cancellation. I understand their chants about daily bread being more important than a Shakira performance, and I have to admit they are right. Selfishly, though, I would miss Mawazine: the warmth of my beloved's arms around me, the drums of many nations, the gentle breeze rippling off the sea, and the floating sounds around us.

Just as Morocco is receiving praise for its peaceful reforms, as summer travellers are changing their plans from Egypt to Morocco, a devastating bomb in Marrakesh takes sixteen lives and damages many others. I watch on my screen, as the king surveys the scene. He walks past a black boot, alone on the sidewalk outside of the Argana Café. Now the loss of Mawazine becomes a trifle, and my heart breaks at the end of a peaceful illusion.

Daoud's proposal

"Mama! Susan and I have been planning something very special for you. Come, Susan. We need to share this together." Daoud feels so happy to make this announcement to his mother. He hopes his wife feels the same.

Susan does feel a certain amount of pleasure at this moment, but she is ashamed to note that her joy is somewhat forced. She has long struggled to overcome her feelings about her mother-in-law. There have been misunderstandings in the past, jealousies, resentments, and always, in the end, Susan finds herself on the wrong side. Again and again she has had to say something like: "Khadija's love is so strange. Why did she think I would want this?"

Susan wishes she could feel pure joy at Daoud's proposal, but her feelings are mixed.

"What is it, Daoud?" Sometimes his mother is like a little girl. At the mention of a surprise, her eyes shine with anticipation.

"Mama, we are very happy to tell you that I am prepared to take you on a pilgrimage to Mecca this year. We have prayed about this, Mama, and if God wills it, we will go."

Daoud has been expecting an enthusiastic response, but it doesn't come. "Do you mean for all of us to go, Daoud?"

"No, Mama, not all. Just us. You and me."

"Daoud, no. I appreciate this generous offer. Thanks be to God, you have always been such a thoughtful son. But I cannot accept. Leave the children here with me and take Susan to Mecca, please."

This response disappoints Daoud, but it devastates Susan. She feels her face colouring, and she is again reminded of those early days, times when she had been so angry, and it hadn't been anyone's fault, but there had been faults, fissures large and small that could now be blamed on language or cultural expectations or good intentions gone awry. Susan feels intense regret and anxiety, lest she has somehow revealed her inner feelings and caused pain, ruining Daoud's happy moment.

Daoud, for his part, is determined to understand his mother's response. When he is alone with his sister, he questions her: "Why won't Mom say yes, Amal? Do you know?"

"I don't, Daoud. I can't speak for her, and I'm as surprised as you are."

"I just don't get it. This is an obligation of every Muslim. She isn't making sense."

"It isn't an obligation if it is a hardship, Daoud."

"How is it a hardship? We have saved our money for this. All she needs to do is pack her things."

"I'm sorry, Daoud. I thought she would be excited to go with you."

"It is Hajj. She and Dad always meant to go."

"She says her joints are always sore. She has trouble walking long distances. She's getting older, you know. You aren't here to see it, but she doesn't have as much energy as she used to."

"I know she's getting older, Amal, but that should convince her to go now rather than wait even longer."

"It's going to be hard for her."

"But the Saudis have special accommodations for elderly pilgrims."

"Maybe you should take Umrah instead. Think of the crowds during Hajj, Daoud. Last year some of the pilgrims from Morocco died at Hajj. Maybe she's scared."

"I wouldn't let anything happen to her. I would be there with her every minute."

"Maybe she's worried about you, Daoud. What would Susan do if something happened to you?"

"Amal, that's ridiculous. This is Hajj."

Daoud is hurt by his mother's reaction. He feels rejected and upset. He wonders if she resents his absence from home, especially since his father's death. Her decision, being inexplicable to him, seems potentially malleable, so he presses on. But the more he asks, the more firm her resolve. His entreaties take on a desperate tone: "Mama, please! Think of my father! He would be so disappointed."

At these hurtful words, his mother turns away from him, and Daoud feels shame for invoking his father's memory in this way. Daoud, who has always known his mother, who could predict her every movement and response since his childhood, feels lost and hopeless. If he can no longer read his mother's thoughts, what more has he lost? Is she drifting away from him? Will Susan also drift away? Will he one day feel alienated from his children?

Anxious thoughts toss and turn him through the night and keep him from sleeping. He looks around the room at all the people he loves, all sleeping together along the cushions that line the walls of the room. Here they are, all together, not like in New York, where each child sleeps alone in a big bedroom, but all in one room, breathing in a unison rhythm. He wonders if they are dreaming the same dreams as they lie, head to head and toe to toe, around the room together.

Once, at home in New York, he heard his son describing these sleeping arrangements to his friends. He hears one boy say that it sounds exactly like camping in the Adirondacks. The comparison upsets Adel, who has never been camping and who desperately wants to go. "It's not the same at all!" He almost shouts at his friend, and Adel's big sister Salma rushes to his rescue. Daoud remembers listening as Salma describes her grandmother's home with great tenderness to her brother's young friends, and Daoud realises then how the children look forward to these visits – not just to see people and places, but to be close to their parents and relatives – to breathe together and even dream the same dreams. Comforted now from his immediate concerns, Daoud is able to drift into a deep and restful sleep.

Mahmoud's decision

When Mahmoud arrives in Rabat, he finds Elizabeth waiting for him in the hotel lobby. The sight of her there, waiting for him, affects Mahmoud profoundly. He runs to her, grateful for someone who loves him as he is. Overcome by the pain of Zahra's rejection, he clutches at Elizabeth. He feels that he cannot lose her. In a blur of words, he proposes to her: "Please Elizabeth," he cries, "Please marry me. We will be so happy together forever. I want you to stay here with me, and I can't take no for an answer. Cancel your return flight, Elizabeth. Please. We will go now to register our marriage, and then we will tell my mother. She will be so happy for us."

Elizabeth has never expected to hear these words from any man. She has come to regard marriage as a bunch of sour grapes. However, these words from Mahmoud disable her defences, and she readily agrees to his proposal.

Don't judge her: she is overcome by emotion, and he is so passionate that he seems sincere. His words suggest an eternal commitment, and who can resist such a thing?

The truth is that Elizabeth is deceived. She still holds to the images that Mahmoud created for her before they met. These dreams they created together are still hers, and she still believes in them, especially the one about living in Tamri near the sea, waking every morning in love, painting all day while he teaches his classes, eating their evening meal together as the sun sets behind them. He would write love poems to her. He had promised that. Perhaps he would write one now.

heArtblog, Sept 25

I had always dreamed of a fancy wedding. You know what I mean – where I become a pampered and pretty princess for at least one day, all covered in frills and lace and tulle, but we have neither time nor money for such a thing, and we are going to live instead on our love.

When Mahmoud proposed, in his eyes there was such love and feeling it seemed like he might cry of happiness. That's enough for me, enough to make me feel like a princess. We quickly registered our names together as married, and I can't believe how easy it is to go from plain Elizabeth, alone in this world, to married Elizabeth, partner for life to a wonderful man.

What matters

On the day before he and his family return to New York, Daoud is hoping to spend a little time with his mother away from the children. The children love their grandmother loudly and incessantly, always clamouring for her attention. She loves them back just as enthusiastically. Because she has so little time with them, she wants to teach them all she can: she must help them with their prayers, she must teach them to cook in the Moroccan way, she must take them to visit every one of their relatives, she must introduce them to Moroccan music and art and sport and wildlife and every nuance of language. Last year, when the young prince, Moulay Rachid, opened a new zoo in Rabat, Khadija had started planning so that the children could spend some time in the capital near the sea. The list of things Khadija must do for the children seems to get longer each time that they visit.

But the time of their trip is drawing to a close, and Daoud needs to talk with his mother. He invites her to visit the cemetery with him, to see his father's grave. When they arrive at the gate, they pay alms to the women outside; when they cross the threshold into the walled cemetery, they pay alms again to the men at the entrance.

Daoud looks for the men who will recite the Qur'an for his father, but he doesn't see anyone. This cemetery is very different from the place where Susan's father is buried, with its carefully manicured lawns and ostentatious headstones. In Islam, a grave should be modest and ephemeral. The gravesites are simple and scarcely marked.

Bodies are buried in harmony with the natural world. Today it is difficult to find his father's place, as the weeds have grown high since the last rainy season. They have to rely on memory rather than vision to find it.

Daoud and his mother stand in the hot afternoon sun, quietly reflecting on their own memories – some of which overlap with one another, some that are uniquely their own. After some time passes, Daoud's mother speaks in a low voice: "My son, after your father died, I had an extraordinary dream. I have never told anyone this, but I am going to tell you now. I hope your father will forgive me."

Daoud takes a quick breath, torn between wanting to know and not wanting to cause a rift between his parents.

"Mama, don't tell me. Don't go against my father to tell me."

"No, Daoud. I think your father would understand. Your plan to take me on the Hajj would make your father very proud of you, but my dream will help you understand why I can't go."

"Mama, it's all right. I do understand. I didn't realise you were having such trouble walking. I really didn't know. I know that the Prophet, peace be upon him, would not want the pilgrimage to be a hardship. He tells us that we should not go if the journey might be a burden. Mama, please forgive me for insisting."

"Listen, my son. You aren't listening to me. I have been giving you excuses – good excuses, but not reasons. Now let me tell you truly."

Daoud waits, curious now about his mother's story.

"In the time after your father died, I had a dream."

"Mama, you don't have to—"

"I want to tell you, Daoud. In my dream, your father came to me, all dressed in Imrah, in a beautiful white robe, and a white cap on his head. He looked so young and handsome, Daoud, and I began to cry. He told me not to cry but rather to follow him. In my dream, Daoud, I became young again also, and I followed him on light feet. I was happy and sad at the same time, and I was excited to walk with your father again.

"He spoke to me, Daoud, and he told me how deeply he had always loved me, even from my childhood, and how he begged his parents to consider me for his bride. He told me he was nervous and excited to approach my father for my hand. I was surprised, Daoud, as your father always seemed strong and confident to me. I never felt worthy of him, and I never imagined he was nervous to approach my family for marriage.

"In my dream, he took my hand. He walked by my side, and at once, there before us, was the Sacred Mosque in Mecca. We began to walk around the Sacred House, the Kab'ah, the centre of Islam, built by Ibrahim so many centuries ago. My son, I was weeping openly. I was ashamed by my tears, but your father laughed and wiped my cheeks.

"As we walked together, we made our supplications. We asked God to unite us and bestow many blessings upon our children, grandchildren, family members, neighbours. We were not talking, Daoud, but we could hear one another's thoughts.

"As we approached the Black Stone to kiss it, it felt strange to be holding his hand in public, but he held it firmly. There were dense crowds, but they did not impede us. We were able to reach the stone easily. As we walked to Safa and Marwa we discussed our life together. Umar reminded me of many special moments: the births of our two children, your circumcision, Amal's determination to finish school and become a teacher, meeting Susan for the first time, how we waited for your phone calls to tell us of the births of our grandchildren.

"As we walked, my dear son, we considered our lives together, and we felt the gravity of all we have done – both good and bad. He asked me then to attend to our neighbours, to look after his sister, and to care for our grandchildren, assuring they understand our faith and the requirements of Islam.

"Daoud, we weren't always attentive to our faith. Of course we always fasted as we should, and your father never missed Friday prayers at the mosque. But the Prophet, peace be upon him, commands us to be charitable with our neighbours, and I have often engaged in their gossip. We are supposed to be unselfish with our material goods and our time; we are supposed to be thoughtful and forgiving. I fear that I have not been as kind and charitable as I should. But thankfully this dream has helped me: as the pilgrimage changes people, this dream changed me, too.

"Your father and I completed the Hajj together, Daoud, as we always planned to do. We threw stones at the devil, and we made our sacrifice at Mina. Perhaps you think this dream isn't a sufficient Hajj, my son, but for me it is. I always wanted to take the Hajj with your father, Daoud, and we have.

"Please, Daoud, take Susan before the time runs out for you. Don't wait for the children to grow older. Leave them with me instead. Susan is a dedicated Muslimah and a good wife to you.

"My son, even if it was only a dream, my pilgrimage transformed me. I am a new person. Since my dream, I have found it easy to meet my obligations of prayer; I have a new joy in my heart to share with my family and neighbours. I am no longer fearful about anything: I just thank God and trust in my future. Do you think I am miserable without my husband? I miss him every moment, but I am not miserable. Our marriage is still my strength, and God is the centre of it.

"Go to Mecca, please, and pray for your parents. When you return, I will be proud to call you hajj Daoud. Do you know the story of the ant with the broken leg that wanted to travel to Mecca from Marrakesh? God made it easy when he saw the ant's determination. The ant simply crawled into the suitcase of a pilgrim to see what there might be to eat, and then a few days later, he found himself in front of the Kab'ah.

"God is good to us, Daoud. If we make up our minds to follow God's path, God carries us most of the way. Don't think about my Hajj anymore, my son. I was there, and it was glorious. Now make up your mind to take Susan, and God will make the path easy for you."

Daoud smiles and takes his mother's hand. He is overcome once again by the joy of being this woman's son, that woman's husband, another woman's brother. He feels God has given him more blessings than he could ever deserve. He looks again where his father was laid to rest, and he says a prayer of thanks.

He hears chanting coming closer from a distance, "Our God, make us faithful to you and from our descendants a faithful nation, and show us your ways and redeem us, oh God, our redeemer, oh God, the merciful."

When he looks up, he sees the men who will recite the Qur'an for his family. He walks to them, pays the requested alms, and stands back to listen, tears coming to his eyes, as one after the other the men take up the harmonious chant of Qur'anic verses. These prayers are not meant for his father – a person who has died is in God's hands and needs no intercession. Rather, the prayers are meant to give strength, resilience, and comfort to the living, and Daoud feels the words enter him in just that way.

He feels a stirring within him, and he is not certain of the source, but he knows that he will never forget this moment, standing next to his mother, feeling a sense of peace — not just a peace of warmth and security, but a peace that is sharp and strong.

Elizabeth, lost and found

Relationships vary by dynamism, elasticity, and endurance: sometimes they are as solid as the walls of the Kasbah; sometimes they crumble, sandcastles under the waves. When Elizabeth and Mahmoud return to Essouaira they announce their marriage. Mahmoud's mother, far from being happy for them, is plainly upset. She has only one son, and she is not pleased to hear that he skulked off to elope, as if his marriage were of no great import. Elizabeth understands, if not the words, at least the tone of the discussion, and she is disappointed to hear the words come from the mother when no such idea had even occurred to the son.

Mahmoud's father is equally distressed: "What will they say about me in my own café," he complains. Disregarding their son's protests, Mahmoud's parents begin to plan a large wedding. The fact that they own a café solves many of the logistical problems quite easily. The family will host a meal in the ample space of the café, musicians will play, and Elizabeth will wear three different dresses belonging to Mahmoud's aunt. While a formal Moroccan wedding requires seven changes of clothing to represent each regional dress of Morocco, it is also typical for brides to wear fewer: this simplified version of the traditional wedding is perfectly acceptable. Of course, they will rent an Amarya so that Elizabeth can be carried aloft on the shoulders of four men. The Amarya resembles a very small castle, lavishly decorated in white, signifying her marital home: no one likes for this detail of a wedding to be overlooked.

Also, without a doubt, there must be horn players, drummers, and singers. The traditional musicians and words chanted from the Qur'an must be included. Fatiha and Naima have gone out to rent their own sparkling dresses and the jewellery and tiara that will transform Elizabeth into a princess for the day.

The couple will spend their first night in Mahmoud's parents' home, his mother insists, so that the crowd can gather in the morning to hold the bridal sheets aloft and celebrate the blood spilled on them. But at this point in the planning, Mahmoud stops his mother: "We will leave directly after the wedding, Mama."

"To go where?"

"I don't know; we haven't decided. Tamri, probably."

"But why, Mahmoud? What is the matter?"

"Nothing, Mama," but Mahmoud's face betrays him.

"Are you telling me that we will be embarrassed in the morning? Ay, my son! This woman will disgrace us! And especially you, a teacher! Whom can I trust to ask? She can be sewn together, but what a horrible pain, and the skin will tear. People will talk, and well, there isn't time anyway. My son, why can't you marry a village girl? It doesn't have to be your cousin if you don't wish! Just someone we know, whose family we know. Oh please, my son, be reasonable!"

Just days after the wedding, Mahmoud finally delivers the speech he has been rehearsing for his wife: he has thought it over carefully and has prepared, for Elizabeth's sake, to move to New York where she will be most comfortable. He can't ask her to stay in Morocco when she has more opportunities in the States.

This technique has worked before for Mahmoud – saying something that is not real in the hope that it will become real, as if the words themselves have magical powers. But it only works sometimes, and not this time. Elizabeth is firmly attached to her dream of living in Tamri by the sea, and there are no words that could change that for her.

Besides, Elizabeth is distraught by the idea of returning to the States: a signal of her utter defeat. She had quit each of her freelance positions with the same finality, and for this brief time away, she has held the upper hand quite valiantly against her mother. She imagines all the people who will gloat with told-you-so faces. All those who warned her of Mahmoud's true intentions will be proven correct.

Her husband has betrayed her with his assurances that he would never leave the land of his birth. Worse, he seems bent on suppressing her dissent: does he want her capitulation? Does he enjoy seeing her embarrassed? Elizabeth feels hurt and, for a bride, strangely alone.

"I can't go back there, Mahmoud. I don't think you understand."

"Of course you can, Elizabeth. I will be there at your side. We will make it work together."

"You promised we would live near the ocean, like I've always wanted. Don't you remember?"

"There is ocean over there too, isn't there? Stop all this complaining. There is nothing for you here. What would you do? My teaching salary is small, and I can't afford a place for us to live."

"I can do a lot of things. I can paint and sell paintings. I am very talented, Mahmoud. I can sell paintings to tourists. You can help me."

"Ridiculous. No one buys paintings anymore. You don't even speak Arabic. How can you live here?"

"I can learn, Mahmoud! I am already learning."

"Be reasonable. New York is much better."

"No Mahmoud! I came here to stay. You promised me."

"Then why did you buy a round-trip ticket to come here?"

"And why, Mahmoud, did I let the date of that ticket pass by? Why? You should answer that."

Elizabeth is furious, desperate, and soon despondent. The seeds of doubt planted by Susan, Sanaa, and Sophie bear fruit now, as Elizabeth realises that Mahmoud has always had this plan. She knows he only praised Morocco to convince her that he wouldn't marry just to emigrate. She feels sick inside.

When Mahmoud leaves her alone, she struggles to survive her dark thoughts and fears. When he returns, he is able to soothe her momentarily, but his assurances never take hold within her; his loving words clash falsely against her ears. None of it matters: she feels subject to his plans now – swept along by his urgency, helpless to stop him.

And then one day it all comes clear. Do you know how this is? It could be months or even years of arguments, two people, two distinct desires, each going in a separate direction while bound together, until something happens to break the impasse.

"Elizabeth, I have great news! I've been accepted at the University of Wisconsin to study comparative literature! No more waiting around about the visa – the university will help us."

"What are you even talking about, Mahmoud? When did you do this application?"

Elizabeth knows that it takes a great deal of effort to apply for graduate school in the US, and Mahmoud did it all behind her back.

"Never mind about that, Elizabeth. You always take good news and make it bad. The point is that my dream is becoming real now. I've always wanted to study in the US, and you should be happy for me."

Elizabeth hears him. She should be happy for him. There is nothing in that clause about her own happiness. For the first time, she really hears what Mahmoud is saying: that his dream has always been to study in the US and that his dream is the only thing that matters to him. There is no room in his dreams for hers. To reach his dream, Mahmoud will need financial support, and Elizabeth will need to give up on her painting to work in the only field she knows to be lucrative – graphic design again, commissioned works for others, nothing that she wants to do, nothing to become passionate about. She doesn't want to do it. She won't.

"Mahmoud, buy your ticket. I will take you to the airport, and you will enjoy your studies in Wisconsin."

"But Elizabeth, I need you! We need to go together, or my family will wonder what is happening between us."

"What is happening between us, Mahmoud? Tell me."

"Nothing, Elizabeth, nothing. We are making a decision about where we are going to live and what we are going to do."

"No, Mahmoud. We are not making a decision. You have already decided, and your decision didn't include me. For the first time, you are telling me that your dream has always been to study in the US. Now I understand. I understand why you looked for an American wife, why you made so many promises to me. I understand that you are dishonest. I understand that you will do anything to fulfil your dreams, regardless of what I want. I'm not going to the States with you, Mahmoud. I'm not going. What your family will soon understand is that our marriage is ending.

You weren't honest with me about the life you wanted, and you don't care about the life I want."

"I really can't believe what I am hearing, Elizabeth. You are so selfish."

The lives of others

"She hasn't returned, Daoud."

"Are you sure?"

Susan looks again at her screen. She has exceeded the limits of protocol, pulling strings to investigate Elizabeth's return flight information and checking her passport location. Though many vulnerable women pass under Susan's review each day, the memory of Elizabeth has haunted Susan ever since they left her behind at the airport in Casablanca.

"She's not coming. I'm sure of it. I keep imagining what could have happened to her. She could have been raped and left for dead in some empty building. I should have asked her for more information, Daoud. We should have talked to that little creep at the airport. I thought I could just follow up here at home, but it isn't enough. I can't do anything to help her now. This is my fault."

"Do you really think she would have listened to you? She wouldn't have listened to anyone in the excitement of meeting her new boyfriend. Come on, Suzy! You are a stranger to her. You can't save everyone."

"But I could have helped her. She was sweet and good-hearted. She didn't deserve this. She was vulnerable, Daoud, and now she's dead, and it's my fault. My fault."

"You shouldn't say that, Suzy. Don't jump to that conclusion."

"That guy had nothing – nothing but selfish motives. We know that. We could see it. You said it yourself: 'he could have at least taken a shower' – didn't you say that?"

"Suzy, we know nothing about him. We don't know if he's a nice guy or not. Okay, listen, Susan: I'm very sorry about Elizabeth, and I wish she had returned home as much as you do, but please don't torture yourself anymore. What if someone had stopped you from joining Peace Corps? They could have tried to convince you, but you wouldn't have listened. They could have told you it would be dangerous. They probably did, right? But you ignored all caution, and imagine if you hadn't! Just imagine how empty my life would be."

Despite her dark mood, Susan laughs: "That's a very different story, Daoud."

"It is, I know that. But you took a chance to travel abroad, and your parents were very worried about you. You don't know what happened to Elizabeth, do you? Maybe she is having a wonderful time. Maybe she found a job there and stayed. Maybe the guy is better than you think, and all these thoughts and concerns are for nothing. Maybe she's fine and happy."

None of this comforts Susan, but she is running late for work and the children need to meet the bus. Susan is certain that things are going very badly for Elizabeth, and she is helpless to do anything. At times her job at the agency is a blessing, but then sometimes it hangs around her neck as a curse. She knows that a woman travelling alone is susceptible to various problems, and she knows Elizabeth is particularly vulnerable: partly because of her naïve faith in the goodness of others, but also because of her loneliness.

Elizabeth has been caught in a dangerous place, far from her home and resources. Susan wishes she had told Elizabeth to seek safe harbour by knocking on the door of any mosque: even if non-Muslims are prohibited from the inner sanctum, the mosque is still a place of refuge for anyone, and some kind Imam would have helped her to connect with resources and a good family to provide safe harbour.

Susan is fitful, and Daoud understands. Susan's compassion is the first thing he noticed about her, and also the first thing that endeared her to him.

"Suzy, it's going to be fine. She's young and strong, and maybe she's gaining a lot of wisdom. What I love about you, Susan, is the same thing that bothers me, that you always think of others ahead of yourself. Listen – we'll have couscous this evening and relax together as a family. Even if we can't go to Friday prayers at Karaouine, we can still eat couscous."

Fasting

All of Morocco celebrates Ramadan; in fact, it is a crime for Muslims to eat in public during the holy month, even though there are exceptions to fasting for women who are pregnant, nursing, or menstruating, and for anyone who is travelling or for whom fasting is physically debilitating. Those people who are exempted from fasting are expected to eat privately. During Ramadan, Moroccans operate on a simplified schedule: businesses and schools shorten their hours; the flow of traffic becomes predictable. People rise early to eat and pray before sunrise, but after that the mornings are quiet and sleepy. In the early afternoon, the souks and stores become crowded, but as iftar approaches, the streets empty completely. People gather in homes to share the first meal of the long day, and only foreign tourists can be seen outside, lost and wandering, unable to find a taxi or open café. There is a time of silence outside, while the homes are filled with laughter and talking. Then the streets are crowded again, as people gather at cafés for the gossip and at mosques for the evening's recitation.

Imam Khalid Latif at New York University's Islamic Center says that fasting is the easiest requirement of Muslims. Compared to the others – prayer, charity, and pilgrimage – fasting is the most passive and simple of God's commands. The Imam says that the most difficult requirement is prayer. Because of its physical and frequent demands on the body and the mind, prayer is what truly challenges us as Muslims.

I admit that for me, at least, he is right. Fasting is not difficult, especially in a place like Morocco where everyone is fasting together. Of course there are moments when we realise how weak we are, how tired and hungry, and we push on like sturdy Americans while more sensible people are napping through the afternoon. The difficulty of Ramadan, for me, isn't so much the lack of food as the withholding of affection. My beloved stays close to me without touching, and as we end the third week, feeble and weary, we are content to simply hold one another as we drift off to sleep.

Ramadan is not only a refraining from food and physical affection, but also from any vices that are prohibited at all times by Islam but considered particularly harmful during Ramadan, such as tobacco, alcohol, or recreational drugs. For this reason, fights sometimes break out during Ramadan: people who are usually high or drunk during the day become particularly irritable if they abstain from their vices during the holy month.

Ramadan is a great and pleasant sacrifice: each pang of hunger a reminder of God's gracious compassion. It is a time to go each night to the mosque to hear a recitation from the Qur'an, and if you go each night, you will hear the holy book in its entirety. It is a time to be kind and charitable and to ask God for all you need. It is a time to gather with others at night and share a meal after sunset.

What happened

In the end, no one in Mahmoud's family really understands what happens between Elizabeth and Mahmoud. Over the next month or so, they simply pack their things, visit various family members and friends, and prepare to leave. Elizabeth is quiet at the visits, sketching in her notebook, working to overcome the grief of a dream that is ending. She seems more introverted than usual, and it's true, but she is intent, feverish about capturing the details. She doesn't know if she will see them again, so these sketches are meant to preserve whatever visual memories she can. For this series of sketches, grief has been a catalyst, but not a basic element. Instead, the sketches are varied in mood – some sombre, of course, but most are playful and lively.

Soon they leave for Casablanca, and no one in the family or among Mahmoud's friends realises that Mahmoud and Elizabeth are not going to America together. Mahmoud doesn't want to feel the shame of a divorcing husband, and Elizabeth doesn't want the pity or the questions about where she is going. She will take Mahmoud to the airport, and then she will be visiting Valene. She has told Valene about the new sketches, and she felt grateful when Valene repeated her invitation to use the studio. Valene also plans to take Elizabeth to meet with some gallery owners. Valene is certain that one of the galleries will be interested in Elizabeth. Tangier has long been a city with an international focus, and the galleries are always willing to look at international artists who have done work in Morocco.

Because they leave together, their farewells are all festive, and even as they travel together on the bus, both Elizabeth and Mahmoud seem happy. They talk a little – Mahmoud talks quite a lot, actually, and this is good for Elizabeth. As he talks, she thinks about a few things: how much Mahmoud likes the sound of his own voice and how happy Elizabeth will be when she can't hear it anymore. She is also thinking about her own body and how it is changing. She is almost certain that she is pregnant, and the sickness she feels on the bus ride is convincing her that this is probably true. Instead of allowing herself much space to think about this, she keeps working, anxious to create more and more pieces so that she and Valene can look at them together and decide which ones should move to canvas and which would be most appealing to the galleries. She looks forward to hearing Valene's opinion.

In Marrakesh they change from bus to train, and this is better. There is more space between them, and they sit facing other travellers. Mahmoud can talk with them, and Elizabeth is left in peace.

Some years later, Samir is visiting his cousins in Toronto, and he writes a note to Mahmoud, curious about Mahmoud's studies and Elizabeth's well-being. Samir offers to visit them in Wisconsin, but Mahmoud replies that he cannot take time away from his thesis. It is unusual for Mahmoud to refuse a visit from a friend, so Samir presses Mahmoud a bit. He's not the only one who is wondering about Mahmoud and Elizabeth, but Samir doesn't intend to gossip. He really is concerned about his friend.

Mahmoud says nothing to Samir about the pressure he is feeling, nothing about the doubts and fear of failure that haunt him, that look over his shoulder as he struggles to form the sentences into a coherent argument. Instead, he provides Samir with a detailed explanation of his thesis topic on neglected North African fiction, about the philosophic lens provided by Badiou and Bhabha. When Samir asks again about Elizabeth, Mahmoud's answer is a surprise: "I got rid of that woman, Elizabeth, absolutely. I absolutely got rid of her. She is still clinging to me, but I have cut her loose. She wasted so much of my time, and I regret it. She was a heavy burden on me. In fact, I am glad I am free now. I regret those years and months and hours I wasted. I could have used them in various things: reading and writing, first of all."

In truth, Mahmoud is in trouble. No one at the university is charmed by his personality anymore, especially since his second extension request. Funding is rare at the university, and extending for an enrolled student means one less fellowship for a new one. Mahmoud has come to understand that he must actually read and understand Bhabha, not simply wave the book around. He must deeply understand Badiou and the fiction writers in French, Arabic, and English whose work will become part of his argument. His responses must be thorough, careful, and backed by reliable evidence. At first, his professors had been enthusiastic about the prospect of a new thesis on North African literature. They had hoped that Mahmoud would be someone they could recommend to their friends in other universities.

They still hope that Mahmoud will eventually deliver a strong thesis, but they have left the mentoring to a junior faculty member whose job it is to insist on clarity and coherence in each chapter. Sometimes Mahmoud loses his nerve and thinks about quitting, but then he presses the pen on the page and moves it forward.

On the day that Elizabeth returns home, her mother's fears are suspended. Not all is forgiven between them, but a quiet truce settles in.

heArtblog, February 24

I can't yet talk with my mother about everything that has happened since leaving home, so I'm grateful to have you here. I have spent some years dissembling myself, but it isn't entirely bad. I came apart, but then I examined my pieces. I know who I am now, and I know about the work ahead of me. I will never again be distracted by the things I don't have. I have enough. I have colour, shape, and definition. I have movement and energy. I will take my broken pieces and put them together again in a way that only an artist can do.

Yes, I made sacrifices in these years, important ones. I let myself be as vulnerable and as tender as I could, and I suffered for it. I don't know what he gave me, if anything, but I know what I gave him. And this is how I know that I have gained more than I lost. Because I gave to him, I know one important thing about myself: I am capable of love - true and lasting love. I am fearless about opening my heart, and the right person, the person who can love me back, will appreciate what I have to give.

And now, I am grateful for a few things: foremost, of course, is my baby daughter, Sonia, who is the light of my life. My mother has invited us home to live, with a softness and generosity that surprises me. She will help me to raise my child, offering space not only to live but also to build a studio, and this leads me to my second reason for gratitude.

I have always had encouragement as an artist – from my mother, my teachers, many friends, and now Valene, who is promoting my work abroad.

I have lived through less generous times, and to be honest, I was scared, and because of fear, I sold my soul. I created work for others, work that shamed me. As my mother often said, I threw pearls before swine. And now, instead of being impatient with my mother, I am listening.

I'm going to sign off now for a long time, perhaps forever. I need to live without a computer, without the beeps and blips that distract me. Today I send peace to you, my friends far and wide, and just hope that we find new ways to communicate with one another. Shukran jazeelann, my friends, and best wishes to all of you for a long and healthy future.

As a single mother and artist, Elizabeth has decided to do without her computer and the internet. The computer has very little to offer her, and if she needs to advertise her work online, she will hire a graphic designer to take care of it. As a farewell, she updates her online profile with a new picture and then logs out for the very last time. Elizabeth's new picture has been cropped to cut Mahmoud out. She looks very pretty at her wedding, with her glamorous tiara and dress. She looks like a spoiled and happy princess on that day.

After Elizabeth closes her computer for the last time, she begins to dismantle it. She has already taken apart the book of poetry that she purchased in Rabat, and it lies in a pile of loose pages before her. Her plan is to use these paper and electronic materials to create a sculpture for her new studio, an homage to commemorate her past and look forward to her future. Although her new career is to create art for sale, this first piece will remain her own.

The paths of others

June, 2011

Sometimes I see Daoud with his mother,
maybe he rests his head in her lap, or
maybe she massages his shoulders, and I
feel the fierce claw of jealousy
gripping at my chest. Silly. I know
better. I wonder about the colour of my
face during these moments, hoping to
keep my secret, my pale skin turning
pink.

And Daoud knows me too well, so I can't
keep a secret from him for long. When
he asks me about it, I tell him, feeling
foolish. It's just that Khadija invoked
such anxiety in me when Daoud first
introduced us. I knew I wasn't her first
choice for his wife. And then later,
after a few years, she proposed that
Daoud marry the girl as a second wife –
the same one he had been expected to
marry throughout his childhood.

And it's not like Khadija herself would
have accepted such an arrangement! She
and Umar never considered a second wife

in their own marriage. They say it was for my sake, someone to help me. I lose my mind even thinking of it.

I became unreasonable in those days and frantic, wondering about Daoud — what he was thinking, where he was going, and why he might be a few minutes late coming home. I would often wake from a nightmare, hysterical and crying.

Daoud still insists that Khadija intended the second marriage as a gift to me, a chance for me to focus on my career, as she knew I wanted to do. He says that she had simply wanted to relieve me of my household concerns — the children, the cleaning, the cooking. Khadija wanted Daoud to eat traditional Moroccan food so that he would be less homesick and more satisfied at home.

This, then, is the crux of the problem: Khadija's insistence that household duties are my responsibility rather than a joint effort between husband and wife. Add to that her insistence that children are not a choice. She didn't see it as an option.

Well, it's over now, and I don't think of it as a threat anymore, but it pained me for a long time. I have come to understand Khadija's perspective, but it took some time and some real

stretching on my part. If I can joke
about it now, it's because I had to let
go of my fears.

Now when I have these jealous moments
that I can't hide, Daoud again explains
his affection for his mother and his
joy in her presence. In the end, the
only person affected by this
conversation is me: the chance to
verbalise my feelings and hear Daoud's
response lets me relax and breathe,
enjoy the sight of my husband and his
mother together.

And I'm really very selfish, after all.
Our visits home are so rare, and Khadija
is so lonely since Umar died.

Amal stays close by her mother. They
have long passed the stage of being
mother and daughter and have become
friends, but Khadija's insistence on
marriage and children means that Amal
is still unfinished, still waiting for
her adult life to begin. And this is so
wrong. Amal works every day to make life
better for others. She has a good and
productive life. Why must she live each
day as if she is not enough? As if she
is only half or a portion of a whole?
It frustrates me.

Since our return to New York, I have
been feeling quarrelsome. I miss
Morocco, and I imagine Daoud growing

more homesick with each passing year. What if he blames me for taking him away from his family? What if he becomes resentful? Or melancholy? What if he leaves me to be closer to his mother? These fears circulate in my head, none coming true. It is just interference, just thoughts to keep me preoccupied, sad, and anxious, for no reason in particular.

This afternoon, I had lunch with Lucy – a typical meeting with Lucy, the typical complaints about her husband. He's emotionally distant, lacking enthusiasm for family life, probably having an affair, who knows? She is lonely, I know – not lonely in the way that Daoud and I feel when we are away from our loved ones in Morocco. She is lonely in the sense of feeling utterly alone, without remedy.

It does not escape my attention that Lucy's husband is unkind to his own mother, and it reminds me that one of Daoud's best qualities is his love for his family. I may be jealous sometimes, but this love that he has is important. It translates towards our own happiness. As I listen to Lucy, I feel grateful for Khadija, the woman who taught my husband about love.

What keeps people married? I often wonder. Is it pride? Nostalgia?

Routine? Fear? Could it be love? Sometimes I think that my marriage exists in spite of itself, that it had been doomed from the start and yet somehow continues, an ironic statement on the nature of love. My marriage to Daoud is something ironic - two souls, both free, have chosen to stay. Now that I'm older, I feel free to tease Daoud about it: "You know you are free, Daoud - free to marry your cousin or second cousin, or anyone you wish - you have three more chances, but let them be good cooks and housekeepers because I'm tired and hungry!"

"No way!" he always says, with a laugh. "I have all that I can handle right here with you."

Even as a wife and mother, as a woman with age and experience behind me, I still notice my growth in maturity at times, an expansion of thought to encompass more and more possibilities. Although my growth probably happens over time, it never feels gradual. It seems to happen in swift leaps of awareness. And almost always are these leaps accompanied by humility and wonder, a new sense of self on its way. Growing older feels good to me, at least for now.

There was a moment when Susan realised that she was a separate person from her husband and therefore had free

FLYING GOATS IN AGADIR

will, and with this realisation came a new truth: that she had to allow for his free will also. It was something like a baby finding her own hand and suddenly knowing how to grip and release. Realising then that Khadija's offer was not a rejection but rather an awkward embrace, Susan found an opening to forgive her.

> So many years have passed since I met Daoud in that dusty village, but we have created a life for ourselves. It is a life we wanted but didn't expect. A life we planned for, yet still it surprises us. It is full and satisfying - three delightful children and a cosy, welcoming home. Did we expect all this? Did we really think it through? Daoud would have married a woman based on his parents' choice for him. I would have - who knows what I would have done? There was nothing I cared about except my career.
>
> Yes, we have a union of souls, as they say - soulmates - but that doesn't mean there is only one way to be. Daoud is far from home, and he gets homesick. Not only that, but he wants our children to speak Moroccan Arabic, to know what it means to be Moroccan. We always thought we'd go back and forth more often, but in reality we can't afford to travel to Morocco every year.
>
> New York has given to us, and yet it takes away, too. It gives us jobs that we love, and safety, but it's security

over passion for us, really. It's a question of economics, and I hate that. I studied Arabic and politics so that I could be a force for good in the world, and what do I do instead? Security. I'm a well-paid security guard for an agency that makes everything worse – war, conflict, destruction, tension. And it's the same for Daoud. He never expected to teach Arabic after majoring in English, but that's his marketable skill here, and what do his students do with their knowledge? Military intelligence, mostly. We become passive spectators as tensions increase around the world, and although we're bilingual people, qualified to be of service, we feel helpless to make the world better.

Elizabeth, herself

Elizabeth is becoming the person she has always wanted to be. She has found a path – a strong and solid path, and though she may occasionally rest or allow herself a brief distraction, she won't wander off. She often talks with Valene as she prepares for her show in Tangier. The gallery owner sends messages through Valene to encourage Elizabeth, and she sends pictures of her work back to them. Elizabeth is true to her work in a new way, becoming an artist of bold strokes and colours. Are you surprised? I was. Such bravery in her work now, as she moves through grief and loss into a whole new life as an artist whose work will soon be shown abroad.

There's a moment that Elizabeth captures, first in a drawing, and later in colour. Sonia drops food from her highchair, and Sophie bends down to pick it up. As soon as the food is back on Sonia's tray, she grabs it, spreads her arm to the side, and drops it again. Sonia watches her grandmother, and they laugh together about the food as it drops, over and over again. Elizabeth, from some metres back, sketches them together. What Elizabeth wants to capture is the mood, the feeling that Sophie cares deeply for this child and that Sonia is a happy baby, loved. In taking time with this moment, causing it to last indefinitely, Elizabeth feels herself warming to her mother. Sometimes we have to let people grow, even when they are older, even when they are supposed to be wiser than they really are.

"Don't tell him about the baby, please, Elizabeth," Valene had begged her, just a year ago, and Elizabeth had not understood. "Let me be your Moroccan family, and I will help your daughter understand her country." And now, in her mother's kitchen, watching bits of food drop to the floor, Sonia's experiment with gravity and love, Elizabeth begins to understand Valene's strange request. It had seemed wrong, dishonest, and unfair, and yet, at the same time, somehow right.

Soon the three of them will travel to Tangier together – Elizabeth with her mother and her daughter – and Valene will take them to Rabat for a day of sightseeing. They won't go south of Rabat, though, not this time. Maybe one day they will introduce Sonia to her Moroccan aunts and grandparents, but for now, Elizabeth feels peaceful without Mahmoud.

Mahmoud has made some changes. He almost lost his dream, almost failed his university studies. The situation had become quite desperate for him. Now all the chatter, the internal chatter in his head, his scattered conversations with others, have hushed a bit, become less prominent in his daily life. His mentor insisted on these changes, helped him improve his concentration. Once he could see Mahmoud improving, he began to advocate for Mahmoud in committee. He asks for their patience for Mahmoud, reminding them that Mahmoud is writing in his fourth language, and also that his thesis engages with several neglected North African authors who could benefit from the scholarly attention.

Mahmoud is becoming a more careful reader. He realises now that his method of reading had been selfish. He knew how to read a few words without context, just to think of a clever response, or take the ideas of others and move them around a bit to seem original. But now he reads with respect for the authors. As he gains confidence, he is more willing to engage in dialogue, more authentic in his views. He considers the long history of ideas across time and space, from one author to another, and he's writing every day now, trying to replace charm with humility. He listens, very seriously, when his mentor advises him, and he spends his days in the library rather than the cafés. It's been a steep learning curve, but he's working on it, and he only has two chapters left to write. Still, his mother worries because he hardly ever calls, and she doesn't understand what happened to Elizabeth. As she prays for him, she wonders if he prays, too; she fears that her son may be turning away from God.

Another way

This year, Susan and Daoud will attend the annual Christmas party for Susan's office. Officially, it is called a holiday party, but everyone dresses in Christmas colours and talks about Christmas plans. There's a lot of banter at the party, a lot of jokes about Muslim terrorists.

Susan and Daoud attend this party each year. Normally they try to ignore the insults, but this year they have practised a response that they will use to meet each of the jokes. The words are simple: "By the way, did you know we are Muslims?" They expect some awkward moments of silence or questioning. Perhaps the focus will remain, where it often does, on the condition of women in Muslim societies, with that tone of pity in the voices of others, unaware of the property rights and marital rights that are afforded to women in the Qur'an that are nowhere to be found in the Bible. Perhaps someone will feel angry or hurt or deceived. It is possible that her colleagues will not believe them because the image of a Muslim in their minds is so far removed from the way that Susan and Daoud present themselves.

In the conversational gaps, they intend to talk about their plans to complete their Hajj, and they will answer whatever questions come to them. This party, they expect, will change their relationships and the way others perceive them, but they are ready for this. Perhaps on the way home from the party, Susan and Daoud will laugh and feel relieved. Perhaps they will make new plans for the future.

Perhaps their colleagues will consider the jokes they have told in the past, the words that have hurt their friends unnecessarily.

Susan learned about balance and moderation in her Peace Corps assignment, and it continues to guide her. In Islam there is no space for secularism, as God is invoked in every greeting, every hope for the future, every law and decision. Daily life is based on common and simple principles: to seek knowledge and compassion, justice and peace. In a Muslim nation like Morocco, people seek balance: between faith and reason, between judgement and tolerance, between the material and the spiritual, between individual and community. Yet somehow these are not binary dualities, not when true balance is sought.

What we see

In Northern Morocco, two cities face one another; both nest high above the valley that separates them. One city, Larache, is vibrant and busy, composed of Spanish architecture with hexagonal plazas – an engaging, crowded bookstore filled with Arabic, English, and French treasures, the grave of Jean Genet, an old fortress crumbling eternally towards the sea. If you stand on one of Larache's highest points, at the end of a maze of sidewalks and walls enclosing hundreds of hidden homes, you look towards Lexis, also ancient but abandoned, the home of Romans, Carthaginians, and Phoenicians, all who added to the scene at Lexis, building monuments, plazas, and homes there, many centuries ago. If you go to Lexis and walk quietly among the ruined city, you will see how the ancient people developed the land and harnessed the sea. They built stadiums and stages, multi-layered homes with many rooms.

Stand on these cliffs, and you can feel the same breeze they felt. Look: the trees here descend from the same trees they knew. Lexis is designed for prayer, performance, and protection. From a high flat plain of green rises a monument – an altar. An amphitheatre rises from a natural grove. Military quarters sit high on the mountain and close to the wealthier estates.

Look down from its heights, and see a wonder of hydraulic engineering from the Roman days: a river was created in a path of semicircles and figure eights. Water flows in open tight curves across the land. From the cliffs above the river, it is easy to see how the water was diverted into perfectly even, precise, round shapes. The river encloses circular plots of land so that the distance between the water and the crops is never far. Arched bridges keep the farms separate but connected.

When we ask our guide about this magnificent engineering project, this harnessing of the river's energy, he looks puzzled. He insists this river is simply following its natural path. We don't argue, though we know he is wrong. Impossible, we know, that such regular curves would have formed naturally, creating perfectly equitable plots of land.

Do you see? The most amazing human wonders are not easily recognised – like the forgiveness of one beloved to another, or the unexpected offering of friendship. Morocco has offered all these gifts to us: love, friendship, resolution, redemption. From morning walks near the ocean to evening meals in cosy homes, Morocco brings us peace beyond understanding.

When we return to the States, I miss one thing most of all: the sound of a muezzin calling the faithful to prayer. There is nothing so wonderful as this reminder to pray: to pause all activities and material concerns, to drop to one's knees in gratitude and quiet contemplation.

When the time of writing these stories comes to an end, I will miss it. I will miss the daily ritual of writing and of waking each morning to examine the work – to see what shifts have taken place during the night. But like any movement away or abroad, the time comes to an end, and we return to our customary places.

As for my beloved and me, we are writing a few articles in hopes of tenure and promotion. In the summers we travel around our beloved Morocco, and we spend the rest of the year bent over our keyboards. Unlike Elizabeth, we have yet to liberate ourselves from our machines. Perhaps we will see you in Morocco one summer day – we will share stories of adventures and laugh together. Perhaps we will become friends.

Once a young Moroccan girl decorated my arms and hands in henna. It was her gift to me. If you think this gift faded away as the designs disappeared from my skin, it isn't true. I can still look at my hands and remember just where the vines of green and gold swirled around this knuckle or that fingertip. As I write to you I often think of this girl, and I think of you, too, offering your gift of time to me as you read these pages. Now we will each move on to other books and adventures, and the details of these stories will fade, but I hope some memories remain with us. Shukran jazeelan, 'alaykum salam.